THE DISNEY
VILLAIN

ALSO BY THE AUTHORS:

Disney Animation: The Illusion of Life

Too Funny for Words: Disney's Greatest Sight Gags

Walt Disney's Bambi: The Story and the Film

Text Copyright © 1993 Ollie Johnston and Frank Thomas
Illustrations Copyright © The Walt Disney Company, except for the
following:

Illustration of Cruella De Vil, page 128, from *The Hundred and One
Dalmatians* by Dodie Smith, illustrated by Janet and Anne Grahame-
Johnstone. Copyright © 1956 by Dodie Smith. Renewed copyright
© 1984 by Dodie Smith. Used by permission of Viking Penguin,
a division of Penguin Books USA Inc.

Photo of Harold Lloyd, page 34, top; courtesy of Culver Pictures

The following grateful acknowledgments are made to people who
loaned us art from their private collections:
p.12 Full page, Snow White Queen, courtesy of Steve Ison
p.15 Chernobog, right side; courtesy of Howard and Paula Sigman Lowery
pp.36-37 Pete tackling Mickey, across top; courtesy of Denise and
Tony Ingleton
p.52 Witch offering apple; drawing by and courtesy of Mark Mitchell
p.55 Queen on throne; courtesy of Peter Merolo
p.56 Top left, p.57 top right, Lucille LaVerne; sketches by and courtesy
of Joe Grant
p.62 Honest John, lower left corner; courtesy of Lucius and Jane Scott Chapin
pp.68-69 Six sketches of Monstro attacking raft, across top of pages;
courtesy of Susan Spiegel
p.72 Full page, Chernobog; courtesy of The Glad Family Trust
pp.84-85 *Song of the South* story sketches; courtesy of The Glad Family Trust

Library of Congress Cataloging-in Publication Data

Johnston, Ollie, 1912-
    The Disney villain / Ollie Johnston & Frank Thomas.—1st ed.
        p. cm
    ISBN 1-56282-792-8
    1. Villains in motion pictures. 2. Walt Disney Company.
3. Animated films—United States—Themes, motives. I. Thomas,
Frank, 1912-   . II. Title.
NC1766.U52D5438 1993
791.43'653—dc20   93-4536
                                                          CIP

First Edition
10   9   8   7   6   5   4   3   2   1

CONTENTS

thoughts of the characters if he is to communicate any sense of reality to his audience.

As supervising animators, the two of us have much praise for the inspirational artists, the conceptual artists, the story sketch men, the layout men, and particularly the storymen and the directors. Without them these fantasy realms would not exist and there would be very little for us to animate. Yet our work and experiences limit us essentially to the viewpoint of the animator in writing this book.

The animator is the actor in our films, and the supervising animator has an even larger responsibility in the creation of the characters. In spite of excellent preparation a film does not come to life until the actors are placed before the camera, and what happens at that moment determines what the picture will be.

In our writing, the pronoun "we" sometimes refers to society in general, or it is we the audiences, and occasionally it is everyone at the studio at that particular time. More often it includes just those in the production unit (about eleven people), or perhaps just the animators on the sequence being discussed (about four people). Most of the time it refers just to us, the authors, and what we did and what we saw and what we heard. We have tried to be clear about whom we mean when we say "we"!

For many reasons these films are unique. There is something most unusual about char-

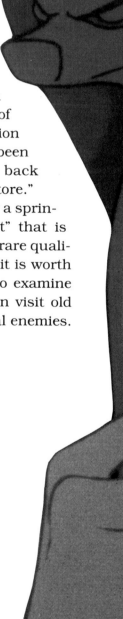

acters that are remembered for so many years. Why do so many people feel that these animated drawings are actually alive? They are only squiggles of pencil lines on a piece of paper, yet they have created laughs and fears, love and hate, joy and tears.

Charles Solomon, historian, author and critic, wrote in the *Los Angeles Times* while reviewing *Beauty and the Beast*, "Fifty years after their initial releases, *Snow White*, *Pinocchio*, *Fantasia*, *Dumbo*, and *Bambi* are entertaining a third generation of viewers. Audiences will be enjoying *Beauty and the Beast* decades from now, when most of the year's live-action features will have been consigned to the back shelf of the video store."

Even if it is only a sprinkling of "fairy dust" that is responsible for the rare qualities in these films, it is worth taking a moment to examine them, to once again visit old friends and fictional enemies.

THE DISNEY VILLAIN

1
What
Is a
Villain?

ALL OF US ARE POTENTIAL VILLAINS. In spite of ethics, morals, codes of conduct and a general respect for laws, if we are pushed far enough, pressured beyond our breaking point, our self-preservation system takes over and we are capable of terrible villainy. Even before reaching that point we tell lies, just little ones at first, we cheat, we may become devious, and say things that we do not really mean and often have to retract. Occasionally we will say, "I just can't understand why he would do a thing like that!" or we encounter a situation so appalling, so completely evil that we recoil in revulsion, but most of the time, we understand the many facets of villainy very well. Greed, selfishness, revenge, the need for power or even the vagaries of the irrational mind are emotions all of us have known or at least sensed, and have learned to keep dormant. When we see them running rampant, out of control, to the exclusion of every acceptable kind of civilized behavior, we are alarmed because so often we can identify with the figure on the screen who is being swept away by such feelings. We watch, mesmerized, as the story unfolds.

Audiences have always been fascinated by villains. Their behavior is aberrant, they are seemingly more colorful than the average person and they cause intense things to happen. The villain acts and the hero reacts. That becomes the story. Whether the villain is truly evil or merely insensitive to others as he pursues his own goals, his victims are forced into emotionally charged activities while the viewers vicariously live through each disheartening torment, each moment of terror, each threatening thought.

The Disney villains had a lasting impact on the public, spreading horror, visual excite-ment and, in many cases, laughter around the world. In picture after picture, the memo-

The queen in *Snow White and the Seven Dwarfs* had a cold, classical beauty which never quite hid her inner fury.

ries of crafty villains, uncaring villains, powerful, cruel and spiteful villains, stay with us, haunting our minds and our hearts.

Where do such masterpieces of design and character come from? Some are suggested in literature, others in drama on the stage, but most come from real life, colored by our imagination and our believing and living with dreams.

In 1991, Charles Champlin, fine arts editor emeritus of the *Los Angeles Times*, wrote this provocative account of an interview he had been granted with Walt Disney some twenty-five years earlier:

"Over lunch in his studio dining room, Walt Disney remembered his childhood in Kansas City, intensely poor and, while still very young, delivering papers in the bitter winter dawns. He spoke of catching catnaps in the warm vestibules of apartment buildings before pushing on, and of stopping to play with rich kids' toys, left on verandas, in the warm summer dawns.

"The memories may have improved with the tellings, yet it seemed to me they explained a great deal about Disney's understanding of the diverting entertainment people craved in lives that were less vivid than his cartoons. The memories, I think, also helped explain his feelings for the dark side of life that Disney could make so menacing in his witches and other villains."

Our own personal impressions of Walt are that his great ability to observe and his fantastic memory helped furnish a reservoir of ideas for his miraculous imagination. When we would see his face screwed up, eyes half closed, trying to figure out what villainous act would do the most harm, we felt he had experienced much of that from bullies in his own childhood. He certainly met much villainy throughout his life. The greater his success, the more conflict he encountered as others tried to take it away from him. That dark side that Champlin wrote about so eloquently was quite real. The puzzling part to us was how he managed to inject so much humor into his despicable individuals.

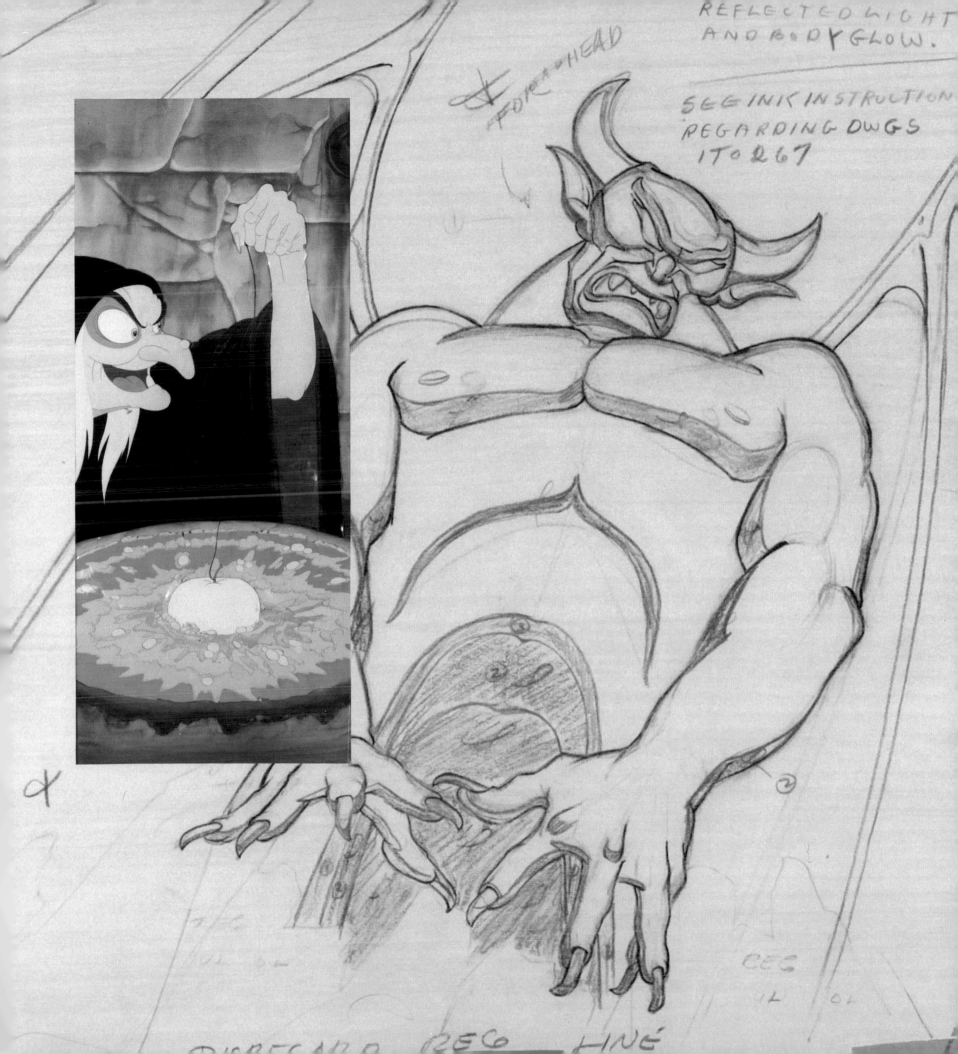

Walt did not like the word "evil." There may be a morbid fascination that captures us momentarily, but no one really wants to look at ugly, repulsive, heavy evil. On the screen we preferred to depict our examples of vileness through a strong design which eliminated realism and kept the audience from getting too close to the character. You could watch in awe from a safe distance, as with the devil, Chernobog, in "Night on Bald Mountain" in *Fantasia*, but you never felt that he could reach out and touch you. He lived in his world and you saw him, as if through a glass, from the comfort of yours. You never smelled the sulphur or the acrid fumes.

The villains we created together at the Disney studio were memorable because they were entertaining. Occasionally the audience laughed, but more often they were transported from their own dreary problems to a time and place which absorbed them with the gripping suspense of a mystery story or the

exciting action of an adventure film. The audience knows that the victim will be saved, but for the moment, the villain seems to be the obvious victor. No matter how familiar the story might be, the audience must feel that this time the villain could win. The plot is constructed so the victim is dangerously vulnerable and almost loses the struggle against a stronger adversary. The tension builds as the viewers watch these conflicts develop.

There are many types of villains, acts of villainy, and motivations and goals that make up these twisted personalities. In every case, the audience needs to know what the villain wants, why he wants it and something about how he plans to get it. The filmmaker must judge if the dire scheme will create enough tension to hold the viewers' interest and keep them entertained. The personality quirks, how the villain views what he is doing, his ultimate goals, and how he reacts to the others in the story will be the heart of the film. There must be no hint of remorse, no second thoughts. The villain is unquestioning in his drive to achieve his ends.

What makes this character a villain? Is he getting even with some particular individual, or humanity in general? Does he want power? Personal gain? Recognition? While greed undoubtedly motivates many dark characters, several of our classic female villains wanted only one thing and were so obsessed with attaining this that their whole lives revolved around the prize. They would kill anyone who confronted them, destroy any device that hindered them, fight with anything in their power to get what they wanted.

The queen in *Snow White* wanted to be the most beautiful woman in the land, nothing more. Cruella De Vil in *101 Dalmatians* wanted a fur coat of Dalmatian skins. Medusa in *The Rescuers* wanted the largest diamond in the world. Everything else was forgotten. In contrast, Jafar, the villain in *Aladdin*, wanted far more than just one thing. He wanted everything — the sultan's daughter, the throne, the richest kingdom on earth, and the strongest magic in the whole universe.

The need to control the destinies of others

will cause another type of villain to hold an innocent individual hostage by kidnapping, enslaving or locking him or her up. The thrust of the story then becomes the attempts of friends to free the individual and the counterattacks by the villain to maintain this prime source of power. Such is the case with the stepmother in *Cinderella*, who must keep her stepdaughter out of sight at all costs so that her less lovely daughters will have a chance at a royal marriage with ensuing riches. This is understandable, for even today some manipulative mothers use their own daughters as a way of getting an easier life.

A variation on that theme occurs in *Beauty and the Beast*, in which the ugly beast, who was considered to be a villain in the beginning of the picture, had Belle's ailing father thrown into the dungeon cell just for stumbling into the castle by accident. There was no master scheme for using the captive for future bargaining but it was an excellent

funny little ways. . . . I don't think you should call them comics. You should think of them as types and characters."

Our most intriguing villains used deception in various forms, often with disguises, and some even had the ability to generate magic. This is very strong visually and immediately raises the status of this particular villain in the hearts and minds of her opponents. The queen in *Snow White* not only had her talking mirror, which gave her the latest information, but also had the magical potions to change herself into a harmless, old peddler woman. Maleficent in *Sleeping Beauty* had even more power, eventually changing herself into a mighty dragon. However, she could not see through the thin deception of the good fairies raising the child as a peasant girl.

Madam Mim in *The Sword in the Stone* claimed to have more magic in her little finger than Merlin had in his whole bag of tricks, which made the Wizards' Duel a very special type of combat. Ursula in *The Little Mermaid* had the eerie ability to take the voice, song and all, from her victim, Ariel, and then turn herself into a beautiful rival and win the

Medusa in *The Rescuers* was depicted as a frowsy, tough, ruthless and unstable woman who had always lived by her wits.

device for establishing the beast as a mean, villainous individual. Soon after, we began to be aware of the complexities in this creature's personality, and the very fact that he was troubled by his actions captured our sympathy.

Most villains become more interesting if a touch of humor can be found to bring out their human side. Many of our dark, menacing characters combined an outlandish personality with weaknesses and psychotic drives. This made them even more dangerous, because they were so ludicrous in desperate situations and made funny scenes in unexpected places. The audience always feels superior to the villain who loses control or judgment through frustration and has a childish tantrum, as we saw repeatedly with Cruella and Medusa, as well as the Queen of Hearts.

None of these villains lost their sinister traits by being comical at certain moments; in fact, they were made more interesting by having some human foibles and comic touches added to their personalities. As Walt had said, "Everybody in life can be funny. We all have

From her intense gaze to her strong, villainous actions, the Stepmother was a hateful, believable, convincing character.

promise of marriage from Prince Eric. All four of these women had limitations on what they could do with their magic, however, and actually became more vulnerable once they had used it. In the end, it led to each of their deaths — except for Madam Mim, who was not likely to die from the case of chicken pox she contracted in her duel with Merlin.

A very important part of this combination is the victim, whose character must be established just as strongly as the villain's. Whether this is a single individual or a small band of determined defenders, the audience must be attracted to them, must understand their predicament, identify with their problems, cheer for their efforts and enjoy their successes. If there is no victim, there is no villainy, only threatening potential.

Peter Schneider, president of feature animation at Disney, agrees: "The villain is the key to your movie and you have to have everyone else rise to the same level . . . there must be a worthy adversary or you have no picture."

If the victim is a sympathetic and appealing character, the audience becomes involved. As the villain becomes more overpowering, the victim struggles frantically, searching for a major response in order to save himself. It is what the villain forces others in the cast to do that will make a story memorable rather than merely ordinary.

It is a lopsided equation: the power of any individual to do evil is much greater than the power of one person to do good. In addition, the villain usually has a plan while the hero and heroine are taken off guard. The villains make up their own rules They never have to worry about whether they are doing the right or proper thing. They can lie, cheat, kill, and live without guilt or conscience or honor. Most often they feel completely justified in what they are doing since they consider themselves to be the true victims of an unfair circumstance. They feel they should have had the power, the recognition, the prize, that has somehow been given to someone else. This wrong must be corrected.

The prince who lived inside the hideous body of a beast had developed evil tendencies through the frustrations of his limited life.

Captain Hook was a bully who loved to act like a complete gentleman, but he was no match for the hungry crocodile who followed him throughout the film. Sincerity in wild, funny actions by Wolfgang (Woolie) Reitherman balanced the quieter acting on Hook by Frank Thomas.

The Queen of Hearts in *Alice in Wonderland* was a storybook monarch, childish and irresponsible in a position of complete authority.

This type of reasoning places an added burden on the hero, for he immediately becomes a villain also if his responses are not acceptable. Animator Glen Keane, who became an expert on big, strong characters such as the bear in *The Fox and the Hound*, and the beast in *Beauty and the Beast*, explains it this way: "If he took a gun out and just blew the villains away, shot them in the back — the hero becomes the villain, because the hero has to deal with that in noble terms . . . whereas the other guy chooses all the wrong paths." Glen went on to say, "The hero's not a boring character. I'm thinking of Jimmy Stewart in *It's a Wonderful Life*. There's a hero and it's about how he continues making choices for integrity and how the other guy makes choices for depravity. It wouldn't be nearly as much fun if the

other guy wasn't there. . . . I used to think the entertainment was the best with the villains and that is why I had always wanted to do the villains. . . . I don't feel that way anymore. . . . [Although villains] give you really dynamic stuff to do, I'm not sure that's what's really the heart of the film. It's often in the hero, and the really difficult struggles that are going on inside the mind, that is so intriguing to me and I constantly feel frustrated that I can't draw well enough to put across how I feel." (No artist is ever satisfied.)

The heroines of the classic fairy tales were sometimes plucky but essentially defenseless and inevitably needed someone else to do their fighting. This gave them time to dream about a future when all their problems would be solved by a handsome prince. Much of the audience still favors this romantic approach even though they admire a girl who will stand up for her rights. Cinderella tried continuously, and got sympathy from the audience because of her efforts; she proved herself worthy, but actually she needed and de-

pended on help from the mice, and the Fairy Godmother, who left her the slipper.

The main value in having a defenseless girl trapped in a situation with no way of fighting back is in the role this provides for the hero. Aurora in *Sleeping Beauty* was probably better off not knowing the danger she was in because she would have no opportunity in that story to fight back. Of course, Maleficent's curse never really affected the girl, just everybody else in the picture. Still, when the whole kingdom was asleep, it was only the very heroic Prince Phillip supported by the Three Good Fairies who could save the day. Strength and determination caused Maleficent to reveal the full extent of her powers, and Maleficent as an enormous dragon would make a hero out of any successful opponent.

The question has been asked many times as to why Walt chose women for so many of his villains. It is a puzzling question since of the fifty-five villains in the films we are considering here only eight were females and each of them was an integral part of the original story

Madam Mim thought she had won the Wizards' Duel by changing herself into a purple dragon, but she was unprepared for a case of chicken pox.

Ursula used her magic to win King Triton's realm and the promise of marriage from Prince Eric but true love defeated her in the end.

The Beast cannot fight as a beast when his life is threatened, but to the end must behave like a true prince.

Cinderella feels that she has lost all hope, when suddenly the Fairy Godmother is there to help win her Prince Charming.

we were using. There is no story about Snow White without the jealous queen; Cinderella has always been the victim of a cruel step-mother, and Alice in Wonderland from the start had her most threatening difficulties with the Queen of Hearts. The rat that invaded the baby's bedroom in *Lady and the Tramp* was the only real threat in that picture, and its sex was never determined. All the historic versions of *Sleeping Beauty* have had an evil, female fairy; *101 Dalmatians*, by Dodie Smith, was based on the desires of Cruella De Vil for a special fur coat; and even the cameo role of Madam Mim in *The Sword in the Stone* came from T. H. White's novel. Medusa in *The Rescuers* was based on one of Margery Sharp's characters and Ursula is the sea witch that took the mermaid's voice in Andersen's sad tale "The Little Mermaid." Although women are only a fraction of the Disney villains, with only a few exceptions they are remembered more strongly than the men.

A weak villain seldom calls for the creation of a first-class hero. In our pictures, if the

story does not make convincing use of the villains, there is no real menace and there is no heart. Conversely, a hero or heroine who is passive, or timid, or too terrified to talk does nothing to help us understand the mind of the aggressor who wants to get rid of these "meddling little fools." But victims who are clever, combative, unbending, force the villains to disclose deeper behavior patterns and inner feelings.

Such attacks compel the heroes to become more heroic than most people have a chance to become in a whole lifetime. This captures the audience with hopes for success, intense involvement in the outcome, and sympathy for the pain endured. Often it is followed by tears at the beauty of the victory, which leaves a warm glow in their hearts forever.

Warmth has always been the hallmark of the Disney films — warmth in a personality, warmth in character relationships, warmth in story construction. This is what put heart in the pictures. Just as we come to that painful moment when the cruelty of the villains has reached its most excruciating climax, the efforts of the princes, fairies, mice, or friends finally get rid of the villains, killing them, chasing them off, or leaving them ineffective and frustrated. The victim gets what she or he wanted, and as the music soars, the audiences laugh through their tears and leave with happy memories they never forget. Warmth requires Good, and the best way to establish Good is by showing it victorious over Evil. Every film that has continued to be successful for over forty years through constant reruns has been carefully built around the potential for warmth in the basic concept.

An important consideration in portraying villains is that they may be too frightening for the audience, especially children. We want the viewers to believe and be emotionally moved by the conflict they are watching, but there is no advantage in crossing the line into something that is too scary for comfort. They like to be thrilled but not terrified. Reactions, of course, vary widely depending on the age

The hero must fight his battles with honor and ethics if he is to remain a hero. Prince Phillip has fought his way through the thorn forest only to find a new adversary waiting for him: Maleficent in the form of a huge dragon.

Ariel has neither the strength, the magic, nor the experience to combat the wily Ursula in *The Little Mermaid*. She has the full sympathy of the audience, but what she really needs is a hero to defend her.

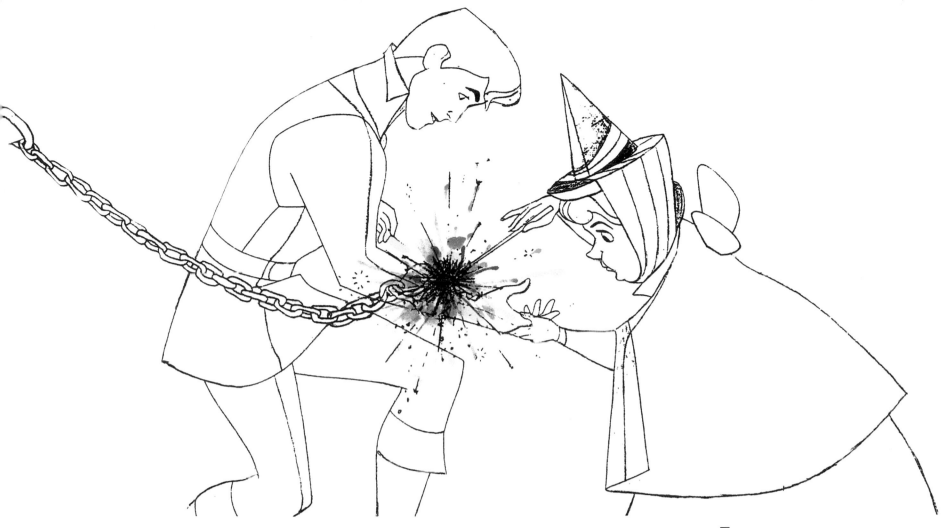

and maturity of individuals and the experiences they have had in their lives. One youngster will hide his eyes, while another will turn his back to the screen and deliberately look at other objects in the theater. Others will watch, bug-eyed, as if hypnotized, no matter how dramatic the situation becomes. Some will have nightmares for weeks, even years, and possibly will never want to see the picture again, ever! And there are children who love to be scared and will giggle with excitement and writhe in their seats and insist on seeing the film again and again because it is so engrossing. This type loves to ride on roller coasters. They will squeal with laughter when something funny happens to the villain, and are apt to cheer when he is finally defeated in a comical way. Then there is a smaller group that become so involved with the characters that they feel they are actually in the story themselves, and will try to reach the screen to physically fight with the villains who are attacking their friends, the victims.

John Culhane, author and historian, insists that children have a basic feeling about fairness. If a promise is broken or a deliberate lie is told to them or to someone they love, there is deep resentment and often an explosive comment: "That's not fair!" This being true, the mere act of breaking one's word becomes an important device in establishing villainy. Rather than a long section that is carefully developed to prove that a character has evil intentions, here is a quick, definite and concise way to evoke feelings of instant hatred from the viewers.

The stepmother promised Cinderella she could go to the ball *if* she got her work done, then saw to it that our heroine had so much to do that she could not possibly finish in time to get ready. In another film, Captain Hook asked Peter Pan for a temporary truce when the fight was going against him but he was quick to take an unfair advantage of Peter's momentary relaxation.

This can also be used to gain sympathy for

Even heroes need help to conquer evil. In order for Prince Phillip to break out of Maleficent's castle, Flora must first cut through the shackles that restrain his arms.

In *The Sword in the Stone*, Madam Mim represents the forces of evil, and Merlin, those of good. In their Wizards' Duel, they change themselves into one animal after another trying to get the better of their opponent. When Merlin becomes a caterpillar, Mim changes to a chicken; Merlin switches to a walrus in an attempt to squash the chicken, but Mim has changed to an elephant. Merlin finally wins by becoming the germ that gives people chicken pox.

The Stepmother has locked Cinderella in her room before the Duke arrives on his quest for the owner of the glass slipper.

an individual who is falsely accused. In *The Jungle Book*, Baloo had told Mowgli they would be pals and stay together in the jungle forever. When he had to go back on his word the next morning, Mowgli felt betrayed and ran off into the wild jungle believing that his only friend could no longer be trusted. Since Baloo was not a villain, he was agonizing over what he had been forced to do, and the audience understood his agony completely.

Whenever the story is living in the minds of the viewers, their imaginations will increase the tensions of the situation facing the characters. The more imaginative the individual, the stronger he will feel these emotions. If the audience is being distressed

by what they imagine is happening, the reactions are doubled, even if it is obvious that the film character is misinterpreting what he sees. We all make monsters of the things we fear. This is an opportunity and a challenge to the filmmaker, for the unknown is always so much more frightening to the viewers and showing explicitly the instruments of terror can easily lessen their impact. Imagined villains can be powerful.

Take the example of Snow White running through the forest in panic after the Huntsman has tried to kill her. The terror she experiences in the dark woods is actually all in her mind. She is threatened by the logs that look like crocodiles, eyes in the trees staring

at her, thorns on the bushes clutching at her dress — these are very real villains trying to grab her and hold her, maybe even to harm her. Whether the people in the audience are frightened too because they are not sure whether what they are seeing is real or imagined, or whether they sympathize with the character and see the horror through her eyes, they still feel the fright and the torment almost as much as the heroine.

All of us at the studio found stimulation in the live-action films of performers such as Charlie Chaplin and Harold Lloyd. These two were best known for their abilities as comedians, but they were also adept at building situations around suspense, mood and villainy.

This was the type of filmmaking that combined personality with gags in a specific predicament. This was Walt's way of thinking too. The villain could be humorous without losing his menace and the victim could get laughs and still be heroic. This allowed Walt to establish spooky settings and fantasy worlds without losing either believability or entertainment.

It is always important to maintain a consistency in any character once the precise personality has been found, and this is particularly true of villains. Even if one is limited to a few attributes as large size and low mentality, he must maintain those as the essence of his role if the other characters are to play properly against him.

Imagination makes both actress and audience experience the terror of this situation. To both, the forest seems to be alive and full of evil intent as depicted by Swedish illustrator Gustaf Tenggren.

Silent film star Harold Lloyd portrays an innocent, well-mannered young man trying to defy the big, tough hoodlum. The audience realizes the danger in this situation more than Lloyd seems to, which sets up the endless gag possibilities.

The same type of comedy was used with Minnie Mouse trying to threaten Peg Leg Pete. Her pistol was dangerous and her resolution strong, but her sweet, naive personality would not let her pull the trigger.

Chaplin used this type of adversary constantly because it made his own tramp character appear smarter. He couldn't match the strength or roughness, so he had to use his brain and agility and imagination. It was important that the gags were handled neatly, deftly. Harold Lloyd did much the same thing, always casting himself against a massive physical opponent or a streetwise professional crook. Lloyd was always seen as the amateur who won by virtue of clean living, innocence, determination and persistence. That does not mean his actions were repetitious or completely predictable. On the contrary, it was just those surprising twists of timing and expression that kept the pantomime so fresh and enjoyable.

Mickey Mouse lacked this consistency in his first pictures. He was often just any character, a jailbird, musician, farmer, hunter, and the bad guys confronting him were just as varied, even though they often looked much the same from picture to picture. His reactions to the problems facing him were whatever made the funniest gag for that situation in the story. He would be aggressive when it was appropriate, mild, suspicious, scheming or authoritative, whatever the story line re-

quired. He was the most effective, however, as the small-town boy from Middle America who shared Walt's own dreams of how an unusual kid might use his wits to survive no matter what the obstacles were before him.

A similar development among the villains was slower in coming. All of us on the staff were quite familiar with many types of unpleasant characters, even a few working in the studio with us, but no one at that time could see a way to put them in the stories. We probably preferred to ridicule in private rather than glorify them and their traits in a starring role.

As we progressed on into the feature films, we gradually found ways to keep a great consistency in the portrayal of each character. It had been a long road and one worth remembering as we began using our animation to create very believable actors in strong, realistic situations. Evil-minded characters from the theater and literature were coming within our reach. Soon a rich variety of psychotic, brutal, egotistical or insensitive players would be ours. By 1937, after a dozen years of learning, struggling, preparing, the full gamut of villainy was finally becoming available to us.

2
The Shorts

EGINNING WITH THE ALICE SERIES, 1923-1927, the character most likely to be the hero, the one whom Alice could count on for support, was a cat named Julius. He was a cat in name only, for all the animals at that time were the standard look-alikes of the cartoon world. For an adversary, there was a surly strongman with a cigar (usually) and a wooden leg, probably based on the pirate symbol cartoonists used to depict a rough and mean character. His name was Pete, but no one knows just what kind of animal he was. Thwarting the bad guy was the important part of the action and the personality of the victor was unimportant. It never influenced how he went about achieving his success, but then there was no clear personality for the villain either, outside of the fact that he was a bully.

By the time the Alice series ended in 1927, Julius had become a definite hero, so he was kept in the new cast and changed from a cat to a rabbit with long floppy ears, called Oswald, the Lucky Rabbit. Pete had developed from his crude beginnings into a bigger strongman, stupid and mean. He still had his cigar but the animators could never seem to remember

Using needle and thread, Mickey ties up the burly, threatening giant from *Brave Little Tailor*, a classic fairy tale. Both characters animated by Vladimir "Bill" Tytla.

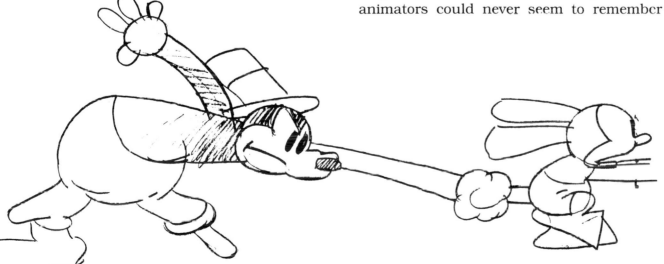

Peg Leg Pete grabs Oswald the rabbit by the tail, setting up a conflict that will create a simple story for the whole picture.

whether the wooden leg was on the right or the left, and in some pictures, even drew him with two good legs. Still he was known as Peg Leg Pete.

He continued to be the villain in the series, forcing young Oswald to become ever more nifty and clever to win the day. With this increased alertness, his emerging personality was happier, almost carefree, and slightly reminiscent of Chaplin when confronting the villain. Pete was not in every picture, but when a strong protagonist was needed, he got the call. He was given a variety of costumes and professions, but he was always the same dominating adversary.

When Mickey Mouse replaced Oswald in 1928, sound brought a new dimension to Peg Leg Pete — a deep, rough voice. Now he could show his hearty laugh laced with sinister overtones, and even a change of nationality, being the French Canadian trapper Pierre in two films, and Pedro the Southwestern bandit in another. He was becoming wiser, occasion-

ally suspicious, slightly more difficult to dupe, but always very direct with crude motives and a heavy hand.

Mickey was essentially Oswald with round ears, a bulbous nose and a long skinny tail, and he continued the growth of his forerunner's personality as a consistent character whom the audience was finding increasingly engaging. In order to deal with Pete's overpowering size and manner, Mickey had to come up with new ideas, which allowed Walt to draw on dreams from his boyhood.

Pete reached his full development as a personality in *Moving Day* (1936) as the sheriff foreclosing on Mickey and Donald for not paying the rent. He had annoyed both Alice and Oswald in at least eleven silent films and continued his rough ways with Mickey and his friends in another thirty-two, but never received top billing.

The Big Bad Wolf

The first villain to achieve stardom was the Big Bad Wolf, the entertaining ham actor in *Three Little Pigs* (1933). He was more than just strong and stupid, being based on those sly, treacherous troublemakers from "mellerdramas" at the turn of the century. Billy Bletcher, the small man with the huge voice who had been the voice of Peg Leg Pete, scored again with his interpretation of this scheming villain who wanted to be so much smarter.

John Canemaker, historian, author and filmmaker, felt that the act of thinking even in this crude form was a major advancement in animation. "The use of the cartoon 'brain' is

fascinating. Without one, a character like Pete seems to be merely a one-dimensional force of nature. But a 'thinking' character appears to acquire sides to his or her personality. The Big Bad Wolf seems to be clever, vain, persevering, humorous — a more interesting, perhaps more dangerous villain. You can step out of the way of the predictable Pete, but the sneaky Wolf could, by calculation, anticipate your plan and catch you."

The thought patterns of the Wolf were always obvious to the audience, and his use of disguises and tricks was matched only by his explosive reliance on sheer strength when his plans failed. As animated by Norm "Fergy" Ferguson, this sophisticated concept made him far more entertaining than Pete, and following the initial success, the Big Bad Wolf was featured in three more films along with the trio of pigs.

"I'll get that little runt — he ain't so smart. Ah — he'll fall for dis. 'Dear brudder' —" mumbles as he writes.

Other Animal Villains

A variety of other animals were used from 1929 to 1938, before the release of *Snow White and the Seven Dwarfs* showed the importance of complete personalities for all the characters. Three films had gorillas as the heavy, two with a towering moose, one with a spider. Other unusual "villains" included an octopus, a rooster, hornets, bees, ants, a whole collection of giant insects, and even an old stump of a tree!

The most surprising was the tiny eaglet who was hatched unexpectedly in *Alpine Climbers* (1936). An egg fell from a nest and landed right in front of Pluto. As he sniffed curiously, the shell shattered and standing in the remains was one defiant baby eagle. He was far from a scrawny, unsteady fledgling and arrived complete with a disgruntled personality, fearless attitude and great determination. He immediately scratched dirt in the dog's face. Pluto's resulting sneeze blew the eaglet off the cliff, but his tiny wings enabled him to circle around and land back where he had come from. He marched right over to Pluto and crunched his nose in the powerful beak. The attitude and walk given him by animator Bill Roberts showed what a talented artist could do with a single scene.

A year earlier, Bill had animated the parrot D.A. in *Who Killed Cock Robin?* who was a real redneck with a belligerent attitude and confrontational manner. Bill knew exactly how tough he wanted this eaglet to be, since the same type of animation on a newly hatched baby bird would be acceptable, believable and funny. He was right.

1

2

3

4

5

6

Cats

Walt liked to be active and he liked to have a big dog along to share his curiosity and activities. He also shared the idea of his time that dogs were for boys and cats were for girls. A cat wouldn't fetch a stick, or play with a sprinkler, or participate in your adventures. A cat would switch its tail, but not wag it. Mickey had a dog, Minnie had kittens. But cats were unavoidable as cast members in films about a dog on one hand and a mouse on the other. By 1932, there had been six shorts with felines as the villains, tough and ready for a fight, or trying to catch birds inside and

the cat world who showed Pluto as the evil enemy and the worst villain of all.

Walt's own dog was a large poodle, handsome and smart. He was not a constant companion but Walt was very proud of him. Supervising animator Ham Luske owned a huge, magnificent tomcat with long fur and beautiful markings. Ham was sure that if Walt would just take the time to get to know such a cat it would change his mind about cats in general, so he brought his purring kitty to the studio one day. It was not a good idea to move the cat to a strange environment for the meeting and it was even more unfortunate that Walt's poodle was in the office for a rare visit the same day. The two animals exchanged quick looks and the cat was instantly out of Ham's arms and onto the dog's back, leaving long, bloody claw marks on one soft ear as he went. The dog howled in pain, Walt howled as he saw the blood dripping onto the carpet, and Ham busied himself with trying to capture his ill-mannered feline as quietly as possible. The whole incident did little to increase Walt's appreciation of cats.

It was Walt's daughter Sharon who gradually convinced him of the value of cats. He would say to us, "My daughter keeps telling me that cats have great personalities and we're missing some good entertainment by treating them like the old stereotypes. What do you think?" A vast collection of ambiguous answers always followed such a question, since whatever we felt about cats, we knew better than to get caught in the middle of a family discussion.

When Walt finally did build an important character around a feline, he made up for those years of limiting cats to very special roles. In 1940, he presented Figaro, the personable kitten in *Pinocchio*. The old woodcarver, Geppetto, had two pets who could respond to his rambling dialogue: Cleo, the goldfish, who was sweet and loving, and Figaro, who had a mind of his own and resented always being told what to do. If he had caused trouble it was because he was like a rebellious four-year-old rather than a bad

out. Nothing was intended to be endearing about these characters.

If cats were the most likely villains, their offspring had a different role. A kitten was cute and the symbol of soft, helpless playfulness and Walt liked the warmth and delicacy of a kitten licking someone's face for an ending to a wild story. No matter what destruction had resulted earlier in the plot from a cuddly feline on a spree, instead of a gag or an unexpected twist in the story, the final scene of six films showed Pluto or Mickey or Minnie getting a sloppy "kiss" from a fearless kitten.

In 1931, a film was made about the nightmare an adult cat might have as he was punished by birds for all the anguish he had brought his feathered neighbors. It was first known as *The Cat's Nightmare*, but soon was changed to *The Cat's Out*. Four years later the tables were turned and once again cats were the villains. Pluto, after chasing one more cat, had a nightmare in *Pluto's Judgment Day* about a very threatening trial by members of

child. The animator, Eric Larson, based the kitten's temperament on his young nephew's and built the personality into one of the studio's all-time favorite characters.

P luto has a shattering night-mare about the terrible things cats will do to him on his Judgment Day.

Angel vs. Devil

In 1933, an interesting use of kittens developed in the film *Mickey's Pal Pluto*. They had been thrown into a well and discovered by Pluto, who now had the moral problem of whether to rescue them or leave them to their fate. Out of his head popped two tiny figures, an Angel-Pluto with a halo and wings and a Devil-Pluto with horns and a black cape. The Angel-Pluto pleaded for mercy and the rewards of self-righteousness while the Devil-Pluto reminded him of how cats had made his life miserable. These two argued between themselves and with Pluto, representing the turmoil in Pluto's mind as he tried to determine what he should do.

Eight years later the film was remade in color with a new title, *Lend a Paw*. It featured the same cast and the same situation, and this time it won an Academy Award for best cartoon of that year.

The devil image seemed like a good device

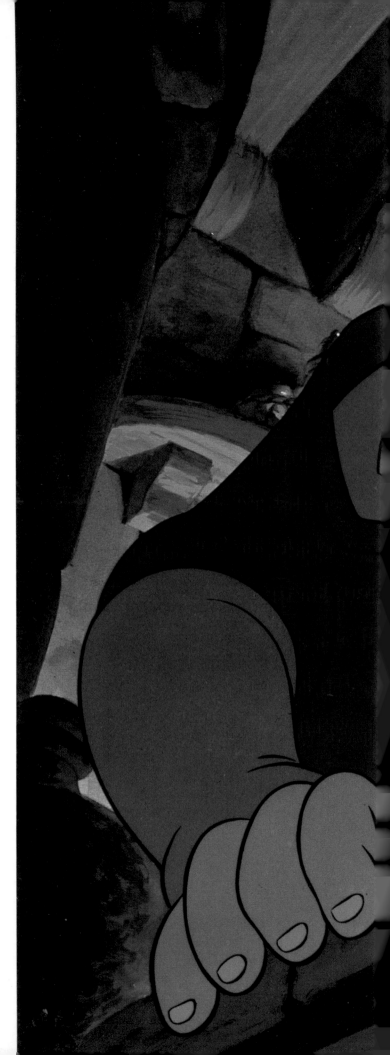

to use in 1943 when the federal government asked Walt to make a Donald Duck film encouraging people to pay their income taxes to help cover the soaring costs of World War II. A similar picture had been made the year before, and while the public loved it, Congress was highly critical of the government's paying for a cartoon, even one made at cost, for propaganda purposes. Walt in turn was highly critical of Congress but was somehow talked into making another short the following year. John Canemaker recalled the film *The Spirit of '43*: "Donald's evil half — a duck with Hitler moustache, dressed in a zoot suit — appears in a puff of smoke, accompanied by jazz on the soundtrack. The Fuhrer stand-in attempts to entice Donald to drink and be merry, rather than pay his taxes for the war effort." No one objected to this one.

The idea of a good and a bad inner self was also used on Donald Duck in *Donald's Better Self* (1938). As he started off to school one morning, he thought it would be a great day to go fishing. His evil self pointed out the tempting reasons to enjoy life with a fishing pole, and his better self raised a strong moral issue and the need to go to school. As anyone could have guessed, Donald continued his education but not without winning a great personal victory over laziness and the shirking of responsibility. At the same time, he was entertaining thousands of moviegoers around the world.

In *Mickey's Elephant* (1936), Pluto was dubious about the newcomer who seemed to be taking his place in Mickey's yard and in his attention. The Devil-Pluto popped out of his head and began to encourage him to get rid of this usurper before matters got worse. The storymen gave Pluto no Angel-Pluto to help him in this dilemma and left him to solve the moral issues by himself. He couldn't figure out what to do about the elephant, but he did have the sense to smash the Devil-Pluto.

Giants

Giants were popular figures in fairy tales and children's literature and always made good villains. There was probably a conception

The b
ideal a
him to
had be

3
The Golden Age

Snow White and the Seven Dwarfs

IN 1934 WALT DISNEY STARTED HAVING his first story meetings on *Snow White and the Seven Dwarfs* just as the new wave of art students was being hired. We were not in those first meetings, but within a year we were not only attending the meetings but starting our own animation. Walt had never made a feature film before but he had dreamed this story for years, just how it would be — not the actual scenes and sequences, but how a character would react if he were involved in events of this nature — what he would think. How would Snow White feel when she is facing a murderer? In Walt's mind, it was all really happening. In ours, it was all becoming very believable as well.

This was a visual medium and Walt thought in visual terms. He would come into a room for a meeting, see the sketches pinned up on the board and start building a whole series of events around the suggested appearance of a single character. He was particularly inspired by the drawings of the queen and the old witch and the depth of their personalities.

They turned out to be more frightening than he had anticipated — not that he wanted them to be mild, but he had never had to hold back on the intensity of any character before, and none of them had ever been criticized from that standpoint. We believe he was a little upset by the criticism of the film from parent groups, although he never admitted

that to us. In any case, he never made another villain that scary, that real, that menacing, and he kept holding us back when we would ask for a stronger villain in any picture. His only argument was that our ideas were not as entertaining as a different type of character would be. He was probably right in that!

The queen offered great possibilities with her cold beauty, her flowing robes, her strength and cunning, her majestic bearing, all from the classic fairy tales. The story-meeting notes from October 1934 say, "Queen wants to marry PRINCE, but he refuses to acknowledge 'that she is the fairest in the land,' since he has seen SNOW WHITE. . . . [The queen] has him dragged away so that he will not interfere with her diabolical plans on SNOW WHITE." From the beginning, it was always clear just why she made these mean, appalling choices.

Now Walt was choosing his dialogue carefully, searching for phrases that were right for the character and right for the emotions. The queen is haughty as she stands before her Magic Mirror with the small casket in her hands. As she opens the lid to reveal the grisly contents, she must convey that she thinks she knows more than the Mirror. "Behold, her

heart!" When the calm response comes, " 'Tis the heart of a pig you hold in your hand," the queen's eyes flash with a new fury, her shoulders stiffen and she violently throws the box away. "I'll go myself!" Downstairs as she mixes her magic potions, she is muttering about the ingredients and what she has to do, very determined, very busy. Then as her appearance changes to that of a scrawny peddler woman, her mood switches to one of glee, and she cackles with the voice of an old hag in anticipation of her coming success.

No animator had ever before attempted to capture this type of emotion in a series of pencil sketches. Just making the drawings with an attitude that spoke of such inner fury was more than most animators could handle. To make the eyes alone reflect the fiery mood was a high point in any artist's career. Creating scene after scene of pent-up frustration, even with live photography and models to study, was new to us all.

The queen's personality changes only slightly when she becomes the witch. Away from her castle, without the protection of her regal status, her servants, her Huntsman or her books of magic, the potions, the laboratory, she is much more vulnerable. She is

excited by being so close to her goal but there is a slight sense of uncertainty. After all, she is a harmless peddler woman, too old and frail to fight back, and when she is discovered in the film's dramatic finish she shows real fear. If she had been all-powerful, the great suspense of those last moments would not have been possible.

As the witch, she is still egotistical and ruthless, but now she is a caricature of herself, being broader in her projection of these qualities. Her large round eyes seem to have unusual peripheral vision to let her know what is going on around her. They also give her an eerie stare that is almost hypnotic. There is magic in those eyes which fits the change that has produced it.

Joe Grant's sketches of Lucille LaVerne as she recorded the voices of both the calculating queen and the old witch.

Lucille LaVerne, who furnished the voice of both the queen and the witch, had been a fine stage actress and also played in early movies where the actions had to be broad and overstated. Since those films were silent, there would seem to be little connection between the voice and the gestures, but Ms. LaVerne played both roles with expansive character and sweeping theatrics. As the queen, she was cold, calculating and commanding; as the witch, she changed her regal voice to that of an old crone, conniving and treacherous.

Director Bill Cottrell and storyman-designer Joe Grant were in charge of the recording session for the voice of the witch, and while Ms. LaVerne sounded aged and crafty with the right timbre to her voice, somehow it was too perfect, too smooth — the sound was not "rough" enough. She overheard them discussing this problem and excused herself for a moment. When she returned, she read the lines once more and the result was just what they wanted. Joe recalled, "We both looked at each other. 'What happened here?' And then she told us, 'Well, I just took my teeth out.'"

Her knowledge of how much to overact,

combined with her classical stage training, created a sound track that was exactly right for the animators. The development of the personality is completely dependent on the sound track since the silent character can never be anything more than a general type. Once there is a specific voice, the character becomes a very special individual. The animators drawing the queen picked up on her personality immediately, and even Norm "Fergy" Ferguson, who animated the sections with the witch, was inspired. Fergy had never done humans before but had built his success on a broad handling of personality attitudes with strong acting in the expressions and crisp definition in the timing. He was best known as the father of both Pluto and the Big Bad Wolf. Now he was faced with a complicated design and a realistic figure completely covered by a robe like a black shroud. Joe Grant, who was responsible for the final design of the character, praised Fergy for the way he had adapted that style to his own abilities. "He was very cooperative — it wasn't good drawing, but he put such character into the animation. Everything was extreme, you know, and it just felt right."

Fergy's approach to animation was to put the character he was drawing on the stage. Instead of wrestling with the inner emotions, he looked for the outer symbols of acting and personality. Fergy even looked like a dapper stage actor with a soft-shoe routine and often made up rhymes based on the dialogue he was animating. He set part of the witch's phrases to the melody of a currently popular song and sang softly as he drew,

The witch was a further development of the witch used in 1932 for *Babes in the Woods.*

And since you've been so kind to dear old
    gran-ny,
I'll share a little see-c(a)-ret with you,
This is no ordinary wishing ap-ple,
It's a symbol of the old red, white and blue.

The villain-victim relationship in this first feature film limited Snow White to a very passive role. Innocent and vulnerable, with the beauty of youth and a storybook purity, she was unsuspecting and never fully realized what was happening to her. The audience reached out to her, wanting to give her aid and advice. They had no trouble believing that the animals could befriend her so casually and that the dwarfs would accept her so readily. Everyone on the screen and in the theater wanted to protect this girl with the sweet disposition.

The Huntsman was a lesser villain because he was following orders and not doing a deed of his own choosing. Still he understood the consequences and many questions were raised about the way the scenes should be planned. When he moves forward with his knife raised to kill Snow White, is he the calm

Illustrator Gustaf Tenggren drew the traditional witch confronting the innocence of youth.

There was much concern in the story department that the audience would never accept such dramatic and brutal action as this attempted murder. Would they boo and hiss at the melodramatic action or would they believe it could really happen?

The audience sat spellbound, believing every drawing, every scene.

professional who well knows the value of stealth and surprise? Or is he a compassionate man trying to commit an act he abhors? There was an indication earlier that he might weaken or the queen would not have reminded him, "You know the penalty if you fail." Would it be better to keep him in the shadows so we never know his personal feelings? Even Walt changed his mind many times trying to find the elements that gave the greatest theatrical force to the presentation. Should we keep the camera on his face as he comes closer; should his eyes open wider, or squint down for more intensity? Or should we just show the feet taking quiet steps, ready for the attack?

Snow White, being unaware of her own

beauty, naturally would not understand the queen's obsession and was completely confused by the Huntsman's revelation: "She's mad — jealous of you — she'll stop at nothing." To suddenly discover that you have a mortal enemy who is closing in on you is shattering to anyone's morale.

For the first time an animated film was truly spellbinding. The audiences believed, gasped — this was attempted murder. As a result, they easily identified with Snow White's moments of terror and her vivid imagination as she ran from the Huntsman into the woods. Once she had found friendship and comfort in the forest, she was able to relax and once again dream of her prince, but that only made the viewers worry more about her immediate future. Having seen the queen make her powerful transformation into a witch, the tension mounted in the audience's imagination and stayed there to the end.

In spite of Walt's difficulties with the story problems, this was a classic example of good picture making. There was strong motivation for the villain, so intense in her anger and evil thoughts with no redeeming qualities, and the victim so childlike in her belief that she was safe. The feelings of both villain and victim were always completely clear to the audience. It was the first feature film for Walt Disney but it has continued to entrance viewers around the world year after year.

The faithful Huntsman will carry out the
queen's orders to kill Snow White.

Pinocchio

The next feature film contained a colorful cast of five full-fledged villains, all males. The Fox and the Cat were no more than second-rate con men living by their wits and always on the alert for a tricky scam. Stromboli, however, attempted kidnapping and planned an extended period of slavery for the gullible puppet. The Coachman from Pleasure Island was even more sinister and frightening, but the biggest threat came from Monstro the whale, who was not at all despicable. He was merely an intelligent animal of enormous proportions with a single purpose — to kill any intruder.

It was the Fox and the Cat who talked the innocent Pinocchio into leaving the path of righteousness. The whole plot developed out of the mischief caused by the very persuasive, fast-talking Fox, who would not give his little victim a chance to think or to respond, or even consult his conscience, Jiminy Cricket. The Fox, who called himself Honest John, had always been quick to see a chance to further his own ends at the expense of someone else. The addition of Walter Catlett's excellent voice raised him from a crass, ordinary crook to an entertaining purveyor of petty thievery with style. Gideon the Cat had no voice, partly because the Fox talked enough for both of them

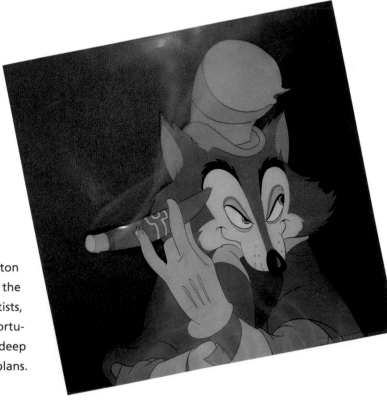

J. Worthington Foulfellow. The Fox and the Cat were cheap con artists, always completely opportunistic but without deep schemes or great plans.

and partly because in *Snow White* Dopey had been found to be so effective without a voice.

Fergy had the assignment to animate both of these villains and once again had a voice track that was just right for what he wanted to do. He had always enjoyed the broad invention and overdone dialogue of vaudeville acts and Honest John was undeniably a type who had succeeded on that stage for a very long time. Catlett's voice clearly suggested all the attitudes, facial expressions and mannerisms that would be needed to capture the potential of such a character.

Fergy never displayed much emotion and kept his thoughts and ideas to himself, but

In this inspirational painting by Gustaf Tenggren, the Fox and Cat take Pinocchio to Stromboli's puppet theater.

this assignment was obviously one of the most enjoyable he had encountered. Other animators might have made the Fox more dramatic, more villainous, perhaps sillier, less believable or more insincere. Only Fergy saw the special kind of entertainment that both the Fox and the Cat could offer this picture. It was the kind of character development he understood and loved.

The first villainous act was to sell Pinocchio to the puppeteer Stromboli. That volatile Italian always gave free vent to his emotions. He was explosive in both his dialogue and his gestures, with quick changes of moods, being violent and excitable whether he was angry or

The animator's rough drawing catches the essence of the strength and emotion in Stromboli's acting.

The theater wagon leaves town
with Pinocchio as its prisoner.

Pinocchio had expected to go
home after the show but Stromboli
had other plans for him.

A story sketch depicts the Fox delivering the unsuspecting puppet to the Coachman on the stroke of midnight.

The Coachman looked like a character from a novel by Dickens.

agreeable. This made him frightening to any know the difference until he was abruptly thrown into a large birdcage and locked up.

Stromboli was alarming, selfish and lacking in any compassion, but there was no animosity toward Pinocchio himself. In fact, Stromboli was not at all concerned about the puppet's welfare one way or the other, as long as he remained in his cage and continued to perform successfully. This puppeteer was entertaining because he was sincere and believable, no matter how outlandish. He was not giving an acting performance to sway anyone, it was just his normal way of communicating with others. He was animated by a very emotional, introspective animator, Vladimir "Bill" Tytla, who had earned a reputation for creating powerful characters. Stromboli was one of his greatest.

Los Angeles Times animation critic Charles Solomon was impressed that Stromboli could be comical without losing any of his menace. When he swings his hips on "Con-stan-ti-nopoli," he is "really funny, but right after that he talks about chopping Pinocchio into firewood. Yee-eek! You believe him both being silly and being scary, and I guess we all know people with a kind of temper that can erupt like that. . . . There's nobody like Tytla for getting this kind of guts on the screen."

Bill was powerful, muscular, high-strung and sensitive, with a tremendous ego. Everything was "feelings" with Bill. Whatever he animated had the inner feelings of his characters expressed through very strong acting. He did not just get inside Stromboli, he *was* Stromboli and he lived the part.

It was only the calm, calculating Coachman who was satanic. It was his foul, cruel business rather than his personality that made its impact on the picture. He seemed like someone from the lowest levels of humanity in a novel by Dickens, with his cherubic face, mild manners and soft talk. He had a master plan in his head but never revealed his thoughts, thus becoming more sinister. He was obviously sadistic and liked what he was doing, which made him all the more scary.

Walt knew exactly how these characters

should act in any situation. He made these suggestions to Fergy for the meeting between the Coachman and the Fox and Cat: "I'd like to get plenty of gestures on them . . . the glancing over shoulders before they say anything and the gestures of the Coachman grabbing the Fox's lapels. Also try for a 'walk' on the Fox's hands as they sneak over toward the bag of money and the Coachman's hands coming in and taking the bag away." These were all simple actions, easily recognizable and fun to animate.

Walt described exactly what he envisioned for another section:

There in the cave, the Coachman, with the help of his bloodhounds herds a number of little donkeys, their boys caps still on their heads, into big crates which are stowed on the ferry boat and lowered into the hold. The crates have various signs on them: "TO THE SALT MINES", "FOR HARD LABOR", "GRADE A - TO THE CIRCUS", etc. The Coachman, whipping and kicking the poor little donkeys into their respective crates, doesn't have to hide his real character now.

The whole idea of Pleasure Island was an example of how to play on the imagination of the audience. You couldn't see anything threatening at first, but you felt that something was wrong and that there would be a price to pay. It became clear and especially poignant when the boys/donkeys began calling for their mothers.

Conceptual artwork in this foldout shows Pinocchio being taken through the streets.

The story structure had made you anticipate this type of climax and your imagination had been giving added meaning to everything that you saw.

Historian, author and critic John Culhane said the most upsetting moment in the whole picture for him was when the Coachman was testing each new donkey to see if any remnants of the boy remained. He asked one donkey what his name might be. The trembling voice replied, "Alexander." The gruff Coachman flung him aside, yelling, "This one can still talk! Put him back." John moaned, "I have worried about that kid my whole life!"

Moments later, Pinocchio was confronting the largest animal in the world, Monstro the whale. The terror shown by the fish and sea plants whenever Monstro's name was mentioned built the image of an extremely dangerous adversary even before the audience met him. He had a sullen disposition, was quick to anger, furious when crossed, and determined to seek revenge against any trespasser. His sheer bulk and tremendous power made him appear invincible. Great care was taken in the layouts and drawings to establish the scale of this whale, and the animation was timed to make him look heavy as well as big.

Perhaps the greatest innovation, however, was the amazing animation and color of the ocean as Monstro smashed the tiny raft and chased the fleeing intruders. Long hours of careful study by the effects department under the leadership of Josh Meador created car-

The animators' drawings capture the frightening moment as both Pinocchio and Lampwick begin to turn into donkeys. Lampwick by Fred Moore, Pinocchio by Milt Kahl.

#32

#32

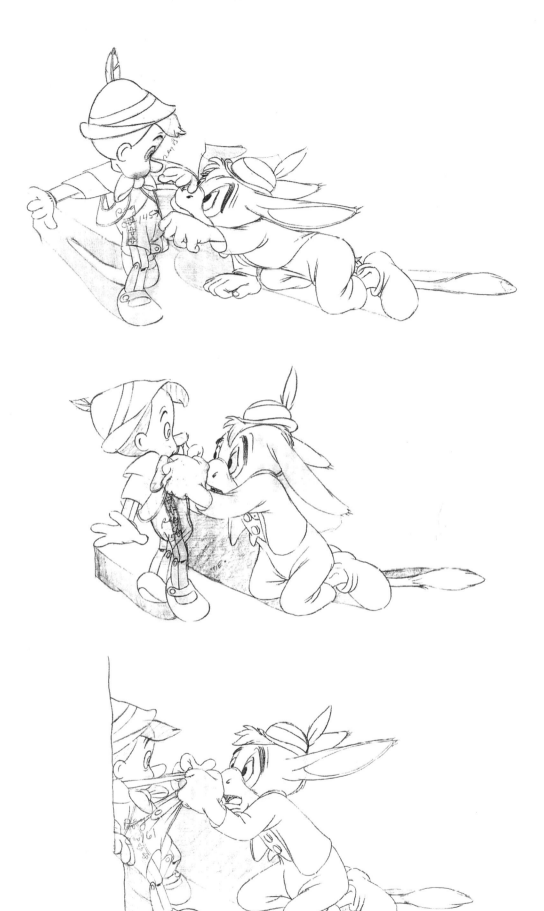

toon water that was wetter and more threatening than any previous painting of the ocean. It contributed the scale and menace that was needed to make the whole situation completely believable. A person could drown in this water. Walt saw to it that the action had the desperation that was needed to fit the artistry of the presentation. "Pinocchio should use every ounce of force he has in his swimming to escape the Whale. This should be built to terrific suspense. It should be the equivalent of the storm and chase of the Queen [as the witch] in Snow White."

This period was the high point of Walt's involvement with animation. He was healthy, eager, endlessly creative and completely consumed. This was far more than a job. He lived these pictures every minute of the day, thinking deeply into every facet of the films, with an emotional drive that was phenomenal.

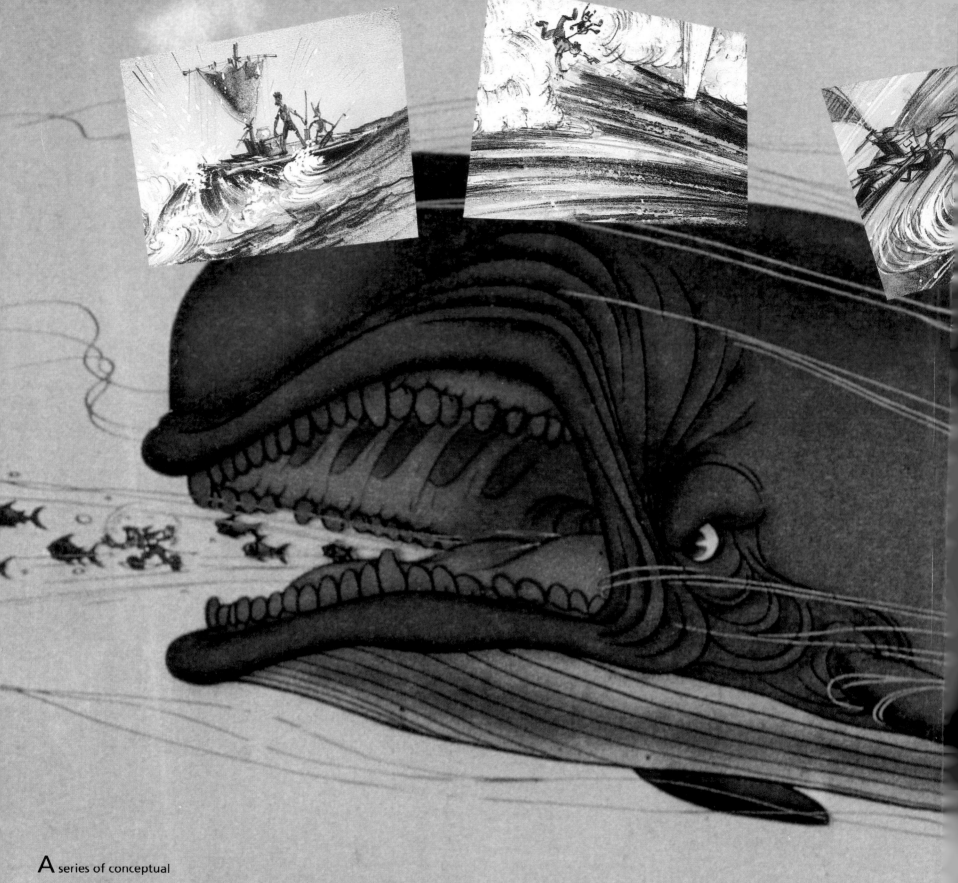

A series of conceptual sketches probes the potential for visual excitement when Monstro smashes the raft carrying Geppetto and Pinocchio.

DRAWING NO. (16)

PAG

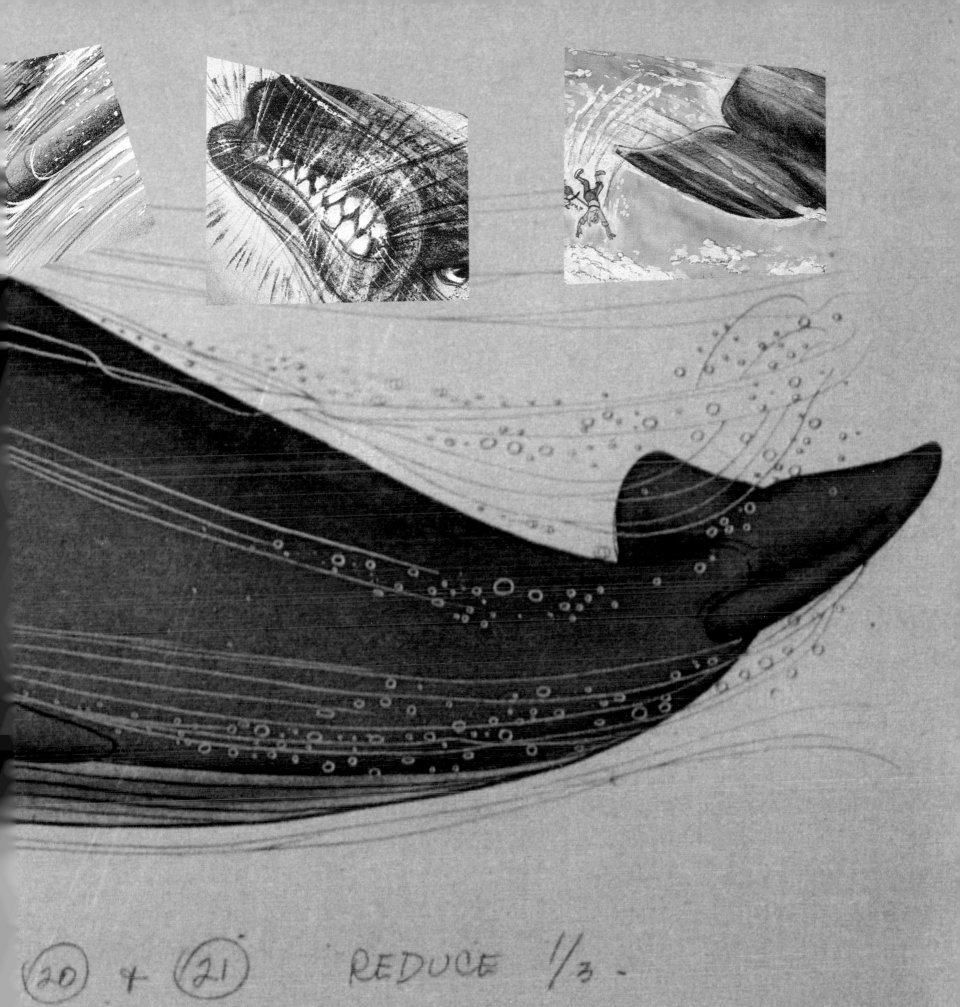

20 & 21   REDUCE 1/3.

Fantasia

In many of the stories suggested by the musical selections in *Fantasia* there was danger, excitement, threatening situations and the turmoil of storms and floods, but very little actual evil intent. Mickey Mouse as "The Sorcerer's Apprentice" was in a frightening predicament when his misuse of magic created thousands of marching brooms with buckets full of water. These were a very realistic threat to him, but it was more an example of Nature on a rampage, like the forest fire in Bambi or the rising waters in the Pirate's Cave in *The Rescuers*, rather than a villainous plan to injure anyone. Mindless villainy coupled with insensitivity can be formidable and often irresistible, but without villainous intent, the perpetrator cannot truly be called a "villain." That requires a mind that can understand the consequences of an action.

Tyrannosaurus Rex, in "Rite of Spring," was a killer for reasons of survival and possibly was bloodthirsty enough to kill out of meanness as well. Whatever his motive, the Stegosaurus who battled him was fighting for his own survival and cared little about his adversary's personality. The primitive sounds from the musical score gave great emotion and power to this primal scene of destruction.

The winged devil who lived atop the highest peak in Moussorgsky's "Night on Bald Mountain" was different. He was Chernobog, the Black God of Slavonic mythology, and while he seemed to have no villainous plans at the moment, he was the most truly evil of all our villains. Others had dire schemes, devas-

Animator Vladimir "Bill" Tytla studies the model of Chernobog's head as he makes the drawings which give life to this Black God of legend.

77

directors on *Fantasia* felt that Bill's Satan "was a deep brooding response to old fears, old folklore, old superstitions, existing in the Russian psyche, even memories of old persecutions and pogroms." No one but Tytla could have given Chernobog the odious, predominantly animal mentality which made him so fearsome. The audience felt the authority of his presence and could sense the mysterious thinking from inside his massive skull.

Instead of eyes that flashed with sudden fury, there was a sensation of churning fires within the eye sockets — eyes that had no pupils. There was no way anyone could communicate with such a being. He was like some

tating plans and the power to enforce their will, but none had the real monster image of underworld instincts.

The music certainly set the mood and the revelry; the visualization is credited to Albert Hurter initially, with later development by the talented illustrator Kay Nielsen; and the phenomenal animation that gave life to this demon was by Bill Tytla, himself a Ukrainian and quite familiar with the legends and beliefs of his countrymen. Jim Algar, one of the alien force that had its own way of seeing, some unknown sensory perception that commanded everything before it. The viewers never knew whether they were being seen at all and hoped that they were not. Chernobog was definitely from some other world and projected an unsettling spell over all in his presence. From head toss, to raw animal timing, to the leering face, it was all Bill's. Those feelings were not on the storyboard, they existed only in his mind.

This segment of *Fantasia* had come late in the schedule to the director, Wilfred "Jaxon" Jackson, with instructions to "get it out in a hell of a hurry and be sure not to disturb Stokowski's music because that was sacred." As he worked with the story sketches and the score he discovered that there was a long passage at the start that not only was too slow for his needs but was repeated later. He asked Ed Plumb, his musician, if the repeat could be cut out. Jaxon said, "He blanched! It was like I had suggested murdering somebody. He said, 'You can't do that, that's Stokowski's music!'"

Jaxon continued, "I got ahold of Walt and told him about it and he said, 'Jack, I'm busy with these things, can't you just work it out somehow?'" Next, he went to the music editor and asked him to make the cut just so he could hear how it would sound. "Not on your life!" was the reply. Jaxon was desperate. He tore the film so that the repeat of the music was out and took it to the assistant editor, told him the film had been torn accidentally and asked him to splice it back together. The assistant was a bit suspicious and quite a bit apprehensive, but he made the splice. Then Jaxon rushed off to find Stokowski, made a couple of quick explanations and projected the reel containing the story sketches along with the music. Stokowski said it looked fine and he had no suggestions. Jaxon asked, "You did notice I deleted

part of the music?" The reply was, "Yes, yes," and that was all.

The finished treatment was awesome and made us all sit back in our chairs and marvel at the supernatural experience unfolding before us. We asked Jaxon how Walt had allowed Tytla to make Chernobog so real and so menacing, and he replied simply that he didn't think Walt expected it to be quite that way. It was the creative work that was done by extremely talented artists *after* the original story had been approved that made the Disney films and the villains what they were. We all needed each other.

The dinosaurs shown in "Rite of Spring" were awesome and threatening but there was more sheer survival in their actions than evil intent.

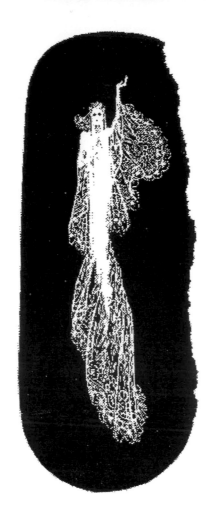

A wraith in a gown of lace. More impersonal designs and animal forms were preferred for the final selection.

In 1934 Walt made a Silly Symphony based on the Greek myth of Persephone and Pluto. He had hoped we were skillful enough to start work on *Snow White* but neither character moved convincingly and the emotions were never believable. Three more years were needed.

At the first light of the new day, the revelry ends and Chernobog folds the wings that hide him from view on top of the mountain.

Dumbo

In 1941, Walt had to give up his plans for more expensive films and concentrated instead on a simple story of an elephant with big ears, *Dumbo*. In some ways, the only villains were his oversize ears. They caused the unfriendly attitudes among the other elephants, his own unhappiness and rejection and the teasing by the kids which led to his mother's being put in the jail wagon. Once again, it was the lack of concern for another's feelings that created the situation, but the insensitivity of anyone separating a mother from her baby must border on villainy.

The ringmaster was unimaginative and incapable of finding a suitable role for the little elephant, the clowns had their own problems and did not care how they made him feel — it was not a hostile world, just a selfish one. Still, Dumbo's predicament was very real and very painful. He was a victim with no clear villain to fight. The picture had a small budget and a great soul.

Walt talked for years about the success of using strong personalities over expensive animation on this picture. The visuals were certainly simple and powerful but it was the story construction and the sensitive animation that gave the picture its impact.

Bambi

The story of *Bambi* was based on nature and one man's observance of the animals of the forest; there were no contemplative villains, only wild creatures trying to survive. A young deer growing up in these surroundings must face the rigors of that life, the hunger and cold of the winter, the necessity to fight for his mate and the need to be strong and heroic. The trials that he encounters are only the normal trials of anyone adjusting to a demanding environment.

The biggest threat, of course, is from the predator, man, and his gun. As victims, the deer have no way of combating this foe and must suffer the consequences, whatever they might be. Man, for his part, has no thought or understanding of the pain he is inflicting on the wild animals by pursuing his own personal desires. There is no villainy in his heart when he kills Bambi's mother, yet to the audience, this is an event that stays with them the rest of their lives.

Because of this memory, many hunters have had disturbing relationships with their own children in connection with hunting. The daughter of an acquaintance of ours tackled her father out in the woods just as he was ready to pull the trigger on a "sure" shot. He did not know whether he was more upset at us for making the film or at his daughter for spoiling his shot, but he admitted that he never hunted deer again.

There was a touch of meanness in the portrayal of Ronno, the deer who was about to take Faline for his mate before Bambi decided to fight for what he wanted. However, it was mainly the fact that Faline much preferred her childhood sweetheart to this gruff, belligerent intruder that influenced

our feelings about the fight and who should win. Villainy was not an important issue.

The devastating fire which provided the terrifying climax to the film must be considered a type of villainy since it selfishly took whatever it wanted, causing the heaviest hardships on its victims. Though it was mindless and had no personal feelings, it was identified with man because it was an extension of his carelessness. The stories from those who have survived flood, fire, cyclone or earthquake

remind us that any of nature's major rampages are more frightening than any destructive force created by man. When it is a combination of man and nature, who should bear the responsibility for unleashing such a cataclysmic force? A villain?

The hunter was considered a villain by the audience even though he was as mindless and lacking in concern for his actions as the fire he had started so carelessly. This scene of the dead hunter was eventually cut from the film since the effect of the fire on the deer's lives was more important to our story.

The vicious dogs that chased Faline had evil intentions from the deer's point of view, but they were really just an extension of man's philosophy. They were also following their native instincts.

Most people believe they saw Bambi's mother get shot but actually no such scene existed. Even this version in which she was hit while out of the picture was cut because it was too explicit.

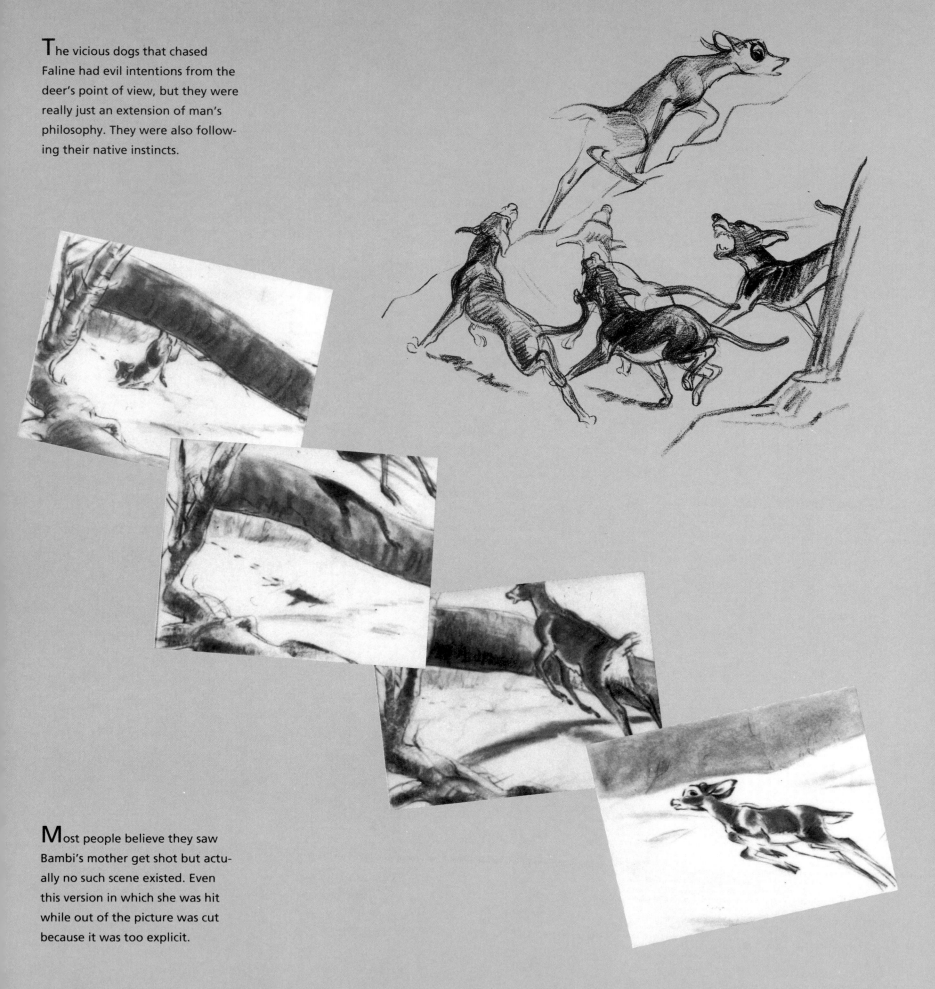

Song of the South

In 1945, the war was over and the studio was preparing two pictures for the market. First was *Song of the South*, with three of the most popular Uncle Remus stories somewhat buried in a live action film, and *Make Mine Music*, which was made up of ten musical shorts in a sort of "poor man's Fantasia."

While there was not much villainy in either of these subjects, there was plenty of conflict. In *Song of the South*, Brer Fox was more than an animal trying to catch a rabbit. He was a strong personality, high-strung, quick and inventive, but so consumed with the importance of conquering Brer Rabbit that he was lured into one trap after another. Brer Rabbit was nimble and could talk his way out of any situation. He was a real salesman and boldly gambled that he could act out a plan well enough to save his skin. Brer Bear was stupid and gullible and easily fell for each ruse.

To Brer Fox, it was extremely important to show everyone that he was more clever than the rabbit, that he was smarter, that he was superior in every way. When they had captured Brer Rabbit, the Bear said, "I'm gonna knock his head clean off!" — which was actually the best way to rid themselves of the pesky rabbit. The Fox insisted that this was not a clever way to get the best of their adversary and so was easily tricked into a battle of wits, which Brer Rabbit always won. They all had evil intentions as they caused each other so much trouble, but none of them could qualify as a villain.

Peter and the Wolf

Make Mine Music contained two subjects with memorable villains. First was the stunning wolf in Prokofiev's *Peter and the Wolf*, which had originally been planned for a second *Fantasia.* Both the picture and the characters were beautifully designed, staged and animated. The Wolf is the epitome of fairy-tale wolves, cruel and slavering, with long, sharp teeth. He had no personality of his own, and was a villain only because Russian legend has him as a bloodthirsty killer in their fairy tales. He was truly a storybook villain, without flesh or blood, and the best example of this stereotype we ever created.

The Whale Who Wanted to Sing at the Met

The second villain was the impresario Professor Tetti Tatti in *The Whale Who Wanted to Sing at the Met*. Willie was a whale with a most unusual talent. Thanks to the sound track recorded by Nelson Eddy, he was able to sing baritone roles from the leading operas, and even three-part harmony where required. Since whales do not sing opera, the professor believed that this one must have swallowed several opera singers, and in an attempt to rescue whoever was trapped inside, he killed Willie with a harpoon. It was not a villainous act as much as a misdirected one springing from his misconception of something he could not understand. The audiences recognized his motive and were quite familiar with this kind of error in human judgment, but they still were greatly moved by Willie's demise.

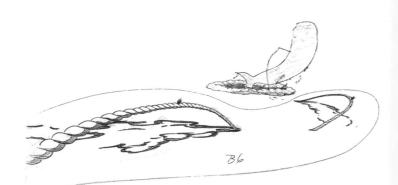

Noted Impresario, Prof. TOMASO TETTI-TATTI, (above) and, (right), world renowned singing protege, WILLIE THE WHALE.

The Adventures of Ichabod and Mr. Toad

Two stories were presented in *The Adventures of Ichabod and Mr. Toad*, both with more conflict in the plots. The first part is Washington Irving's story of Ichabod Crane, the opportunistic schoolmaster. Enterprising, always reaching beyond his means or position and completely superstitious, he is easy prey for the town bully, Brom Bones. When they compete on an intellectual level, Brom is bested at every turn by the experienced Ichabod, who is always alert enough to win each crisis as it arises. It is almost as if he had eyes in the back of his head.

Brom, on the other hand, is a man of action to whom thinking is a painful process. In his simple mind, he is seeking a physical way to get even. The Headless Horseman act and the ride through Sleepy Hollow created a great comic confrontation with neither character being an actual villain. Ichabod was an unsympathetic welcher, and Brom Bones was a prankster and a rowdy, but mainly just funloving. It is the play between the two personalities and the situations that captures us rather than a battle between good and evil.

"Mr. Toad," based on the British children's classic *The Wind in the Willows*, had two scoundrels that caused troubles for the main characters. Mr. Winkie, the barkeeper at the tavern, who had taken advantage of a rare chance to get Toad Hall for himself, and the District Attorney, who prosecuted the case without concern for the victim. Mr. Winkie and his henchmen were small-time crooks, treacherous and skillful. This gang of weasels was a caricature of the turn-of-the-century British street hoodlums, while the smiling, well-mannered Mr. Winkie was the smooth con artist who was never flustered. They were all entertaining without losing any of their theatrical villainy.

The D.A., an aggressive egotist with no compassion, was a browbeater obviously more interested in getting a conviction than in seeking justice. He had an intimidating flair

The dangers in the woods of Sleepy Hollow are actually all in Ichabod's imagination, but the audience was nervous too because they saw what *he* saw rather than what was really there.

and was interested primarily in his style and his appearance. His performance combined fast moves that confused the witnesses with his rapid speech and an accusing manner.

In spite of the high points and new ideas that bubbled to the surface in these pictures, none had the spectacular success that the studio needed to get back on top. Walt had reason to worry. His energies were at a low ebb, he had no money and he was beginning to lose his confidence. The fun had gone out of the business of animation, and even after the war was over, there still was no market for his product. The Golden Age of animated feature films had come to an end.

Mr. Winkie was sly and experienced in treacherous ways.

The prosecuting attorney attempts to confuse Toad on the stand. This unpleasant barrister was based on bullies that the animator, Ollie Johnston, had known in school.

Bill Roberts had animated a fast-talking D.A. with his parrot character in *Who Killed Cock Robin?* [1935] Ten years later the storymen went further with that concept.

4

The Nine Old Men

AS EARLY AS 1946 THE DISNEY FAMILY doctor told Walt that he needed to get his mind on something else for a while — get a hobby! He was certainly ready for a project that would give his imagination a new lease on life. As he relaxed, his confidence began to return and with it the realization that the studio desperately needed a "classic" animated feature to recapture the large audiences. Obviously, they had not been satisfied with the more varied concepts for the films or the less expensive attempts to find something new. The viewers wanted a picture with characters they could love, a story with a plot that could end happily and a villain who could be defeated. He chose *Cinderella.*

The Nine Old Men in their mid-forties, some twelve years after being given their unusual title. From left: Ward Kimball, Eric Larson, Frank Thomas, Marc Davis, Ollie Johnston, Les Clark, Milt Kahl, John Lounsbery and Woolie Reitherman.

Cinderella

Cinderella had the same type of appeal as *Snow White and the Seven Dwarfs,* but the studio needed a far more efficient method of producing it. Walt knew that live action was cheaper than animation, so for *Cinderella* he had us shoot all the scenes that involved human characters with real actors. This film was cut together so everything could be checked and approved before the slow, wonderful process of drawing every figure was started. It gave the animators new ideas on personalities, refinements in acting and communication while eliminating anything experimental or overly imaginative (or expensive).

When Walt was told to get a hobby he chose model making, but had soon expanded his ideas to include a scale model locomotive and a railroad layout which filled his backyard. Typical of Walt, his hobby grew larger and larger, and before long, he was planning a whole amusement park that would be encircled with full size narrow gauge trains—Disneyland! Photo by Ollie Johnston.

In an early story meeting, Walt outlined to his staff what had to be done:

> . . . .the real payoff is personality. If you like the girl and she's convincing — and the mice — we don't have to go putting all the colors we've got on them and running up the cost. . . . Take DUMBO as a good example. We went there for personality. A lot of things were wrong technically with the picture, but still today people remember it. . . . Take SNOW WHITE [and] the things that are wrong with it — still people remember it because of the overall story and sympathy in the character — and they still don't see the faults.

Cinderella was the most thoroughly planned picture we ever made. The story was written in detail, the characters were carefully developed, all based on sound story structure, and the villain-victim relationship was one of the very best we had on any feature. Often, patrons would be horrified or dismayed by the behavior of a villain, but more people actually hated the stepmother than any other villain we ever created.

Walt knew what she should be. "Oh, she's a heavy," and he went on to explain that when a heavy in a picture agrees to do something, the other characters may believe him, "but you look in his eyes and you know he'll cross them up. I think we should get that with her."

As Walt continued to outline the story, he began to search for the dialogue. When the invitation to the ball arrives, Cinderella wants to go and pleads with her stepmother, who says,

"Why, of course, child, if you get your work done."

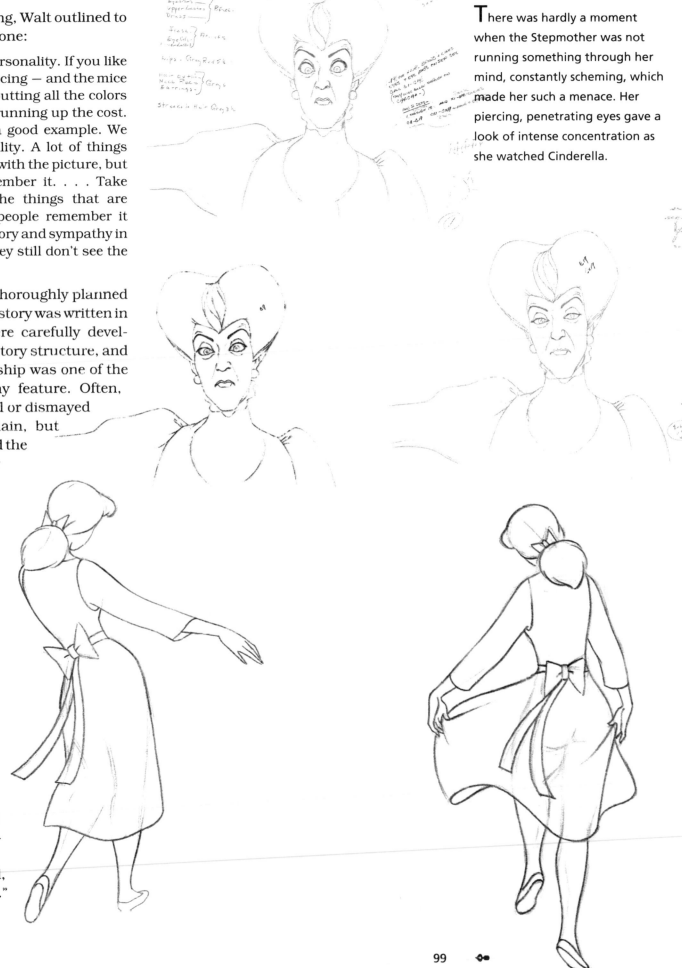

There was hardly a moment when the Stepmother was not running something through her mind, constantly scheming, which made her such a menace. Her piercing, penetrating eyes gave a look of intense concentration as she watched Cinderella.

Every day had an ominous beginning for Cinderella.

The Stepmother lived close to Cinderella where she could daily enforce her will as she made a scullery maid of her own stepdaughter.

Cinderella answers, "Oh, I will, I promise. I'll get a lovely dress too. I know you'll be proud of me." Later when she is wearing the dress the mice have made for her and is running to join the departing family, Walt described how he saw the scene.

> What I see is a beautiful dress — they have done a beautiful job. The stepmother is just speechless. Doesn't know what to say. The child has bested her. . . Suddenly one sister recognizes her beads. Another this and this and this — and they rip the hell out of her.

That's all you have to do. As they're pulling the poor girl to pieces, the stepmother watches coldly with a little smile on her face. She doesn't have to do a thing.

Surprisingly, there was greater opportunity for individual contributions on the stepmother than we had thought. First, there was the voice and acting of Eleanor Audley, who felt the character deeply and had the ability and experience to add real fire to the stepmother's villainy. Second, the animator drawing the scenes kept a consistency of

personality as well as an appreciation of what Eleanor's talents had given us. It was a difficult assignment but a thrilling one working to that voice track with so much innuendo mixed in with the fierce power. Cinderella was resolute and hard to discourage, but she was no match for her stepmother.

This villain had to be "real" in the minds of the viewers because Cinderella was handled in such a realistic way. The King, the Duke, even the Fairy Godmother, were drawn in a broader fashion which allowed them a greater

range of movements and caricature. In order for the stepmother to be more sinister, she had to be more subtle in her acting, which restricted how she was drawn but fit her character well.

She was the only villain to live beside her victim day by day. This brought out interesting rela-tionships, nuances and a refinement that could not be portrayed with most of our other evil characters. The queen in *Snow White* watched from her window and was never seen with her stepdaughter. Alone, she was more dramatic than would have been possible in the presence of the girl. There was an aloof-ness and coldness in this use of privacy; she even used others to carry out her dastardly plans. The stepmother did most of her evil work while Cinderella was watching, which gave the animator the opportunity to show reactions on her young face to the cruelties, the rejection, the snide criticism, the hatred and the lies. It was an ideal way to show Cinderella's spunkiness and her sensitivity while achieving the best possible involvement with the audience. Both characters came off as very strong personalities, very understand-able, and very memorable. From a theatrical standpoint, they were good for each other.

The stepsisters were not even second-rate villains. They were too lazy, too slovenly, too spoiled to be more than a degrading annoy-ance. Their role in the story was to show by contrast just how lovely Cinderella really was. Any further development of their antagonism through their personalities would have weak-

Cinderella's every move aroused suspicion.

The stepsisters could not even get along with each other.

Lucifer was the ultimate self-centered, mean cat who enjoyed making life miserable for both Cinderella and her animal friends.

Lucifer looked fat and lazy but the mice knew how dangerous he was. He was neither a schemer nor a deep thinker, preferring to react quickly to his surroundings on the spur of the moment.

ened the role of the stepmother. All productions of this classic fairy tale have difficulty in making the stepsisters truly funny because of these restrictions on their part in the story. They are left little more than awkwardness and dull-witted buffoonery to entertain the audience. Too ugly and they become gross, too refined and they become vague and weak. It is a difficult role for the actor.

The stepmother's overweight cat, Lucifer, who was used to having his own way in everything, reflected the same mean qualities of his mistress but he had a larger role as a personality in the story. When animator Ward Kimball was looking about for a model for Lucifer, he said he found him in his own backyard — "a big, fat, useless cat" who took advantage of every chance to make the whole world accommodate his desires. Ward immediately saw more entertainment in a spoiled,

ruthless bully than in an ordinary cat with a normal penchant for mice.

Lucifer was a vindictive villain all on his own. Lethargic and indolent most of the time, he was also quick and strong when mice were about, and a very respected antagonist. He was neither a believable, anatomical feline nor a cartoon symbol of a cat such as we had used in the shorts. He was a combination of both in the way that Kimball always made his personal statements. He prided himself on never drawing anything the same as anybody else and Lucifer was a special villain like none other.

Cinderella was not the only moneymaker at the start of the 1950s — new releases of *Pinocchio*, *Fantasia* and *Bambi* finally also achieved success at the box office. Walt still needed his hobby to ease his tensions, but the studio was back in business.

Alice in Wonderland

For the next feature, which would be released in 1951, Walt decided to make *Alice in Wonderland*, a picture that had intrigued him for years. He liked the idea of a young girl living in her own dream yet not realizing why everything was so strange. He tried to explain how he felt. "You doze off and then you dream that you wake up. And that's what she does. She thinks she dozed off but woke up and saw this rabbit. That's the way a dream affects me. I dream that I am lying awake in bed and can't sleep. I will spend the whole night rolling and tossing, dreaming I can't sleep."

A storyman asked, "How do you feel the next morning?" Walt responded, "Worn out."

Unfortunately, either he lacked the energy to make a strong feature out of the episodic story material or he failed to communicate his uncertain feelings to his staff. We sensed that all of us in the creative departments were being asked to contribute more than usual, with those who had worked closest to Walt having the greatest influence. In animation, this meant the group known as the Nine Old Men. (A reference to President Roosevelt's Supreme Court in the late 1930s. When they had declared F.D.R.'s new ideas for ending the Depression unconstitutional, he had called the justices "his nine old men, all too aged to recognize a new idea." Ten years later, Walt Disney, looking for a way to needle the nine members of his animation board, adopted the phrase, claiming that we were all "over the hill," even though we had barely turned thirty.) As for *Alice*, the result was a very interesting, disjointed film with moments of high entertainment and other sections that seemed mild or puzzling.

A quick change of moods was typical of the Queen of Hearts, as seen in this scene by Frank Thomas.

The Cheshire Cat was the most successful character in the film, combining fantasy with silliness in highly imaginative situations, all based on Sterling Holloway's voice and very personal delivery.

Alice was the victim of impossible situations and bad advice in this unfriendly world.

The lack of believable situations or sincere personalities created a situation where extreme costumes and intriguing character designs could help give the feeling of a real dreamworld. These sketches (below and opposite), by Mary Blair had a strong influence on all of us.

Marc Davis summed it up this way:

A little girl goes down under the ground to this world of mad people, and she doesn't even have the cat to work with, she never caught the rabbit, and as a result, she never existed as a personality. . . we missed something in that film . . . if she had been something you were sympathetic towards, or you felt warmly towards . . . I used to think it was the animation, but I think now it was in the conception . . . a little person alone in a madhouse . . . how can you establish anything? It's a cold film.

The Queen of Hearts was another attempt to create a comic villain who would be funny with no comedy business to perform. She was irrational and unpredictable, screaming with rage or acting coy and girlish. However, no situation or relationship or dialogue gave support to any specific personality trait or attitude. She was simply not developed enough to be funny. She was merely part of a whole dreamworld based on playing cards, not really dangerous or threatening in spite of the importance she felt in her own kingdom. Although her subjects were all shaking with terror at her constant command "Off with their heads!" the audience felt no such concern. Peculiar actions and visual gimmicks can hold an audience only for a limited time and there is always a problem with the continuity once that crucial point has been passed. In *Alice* the challenge of finding the humor in such episodes was generally beyond us.

Down in Wonderland, Alice met the most perplexing feline of them all, the Cheshire Cat, which was based not on a cat but on a well-known cheese product. Still he was the most successful character in the movie because he had a definite role with actions that involved Alice. He disappeared at crucial times and had good dialogue to support the madness of his role. This encouraged the animators to be more imaginative and contribute ideas of their own to the situation as well as to the character. No one knew if he was a villain or not, but he certainly caused Alice trouble every time they met, sending her in the wrong direction and giving confusing advice. With the magical, fey quality of Sterling Holloway's voice, he was truly living in a dreamworld all his own.

Ward Kimball had set the final design and keyed the character with a few scenes of animation. He had asked a storyman earlier, "How are we going to make it mad when

they're all crazy — each one trying to outdo the other?" No one could answer that, but Ward was always inventive and determined that his work would attract attention. He drew his first scenes and looked at them carefully. "When that cat comes on and he hardly moves, just the tail, and the voice is slow, and he works his eyes, that would be the real mad character. He was underplayed, underdone. Then it struck me, this is the only mad thing in this crazy picture."

Alice became a cult film at universities around the country where its bizarre characters, imagination, illogical invention and captivating visuals found a receptive audience. Still, much of the staff wondered, "What if we had made *Alice* during those exciting prewar years — would it have been done differently, with perhaps greater menace in the Queen of Hearts and more of a driving theme throughout the whole film?" Or maybe it was one of those films that did not need a compelling villain-victim relationship.

Whatever we did, we felt that we had failed to find the intriguing combination of fantasy, satire and whimsy that made the original

actually far into the animation before we found our entertaining villain as a complete character. He could not be truly evil, because Peter Pan is a story of children and their games and their views of life and growing up. In this context, Captain Hook was a "bad guy" and a "scurvy villain" but only as a worthy competitor for Peter Pan.

He even lacked the simple ability to fly. In a way, it helped the audience to understand his difficulties and the frustrations that any of us would feel in the same situation. His strength was in his scheming, for that type of

In contrast, one director insisted that he should be a complete heavy with no foppishness or less villainous traits to weaken his character. This, of course, did not work in the areas with the crocodile after him since a truly heavy villain became ridiculous and unbelievable once he lost his snarling and threatening attitude. He needed to be an actor relishing his role as a gentleman of charm and good taste, yet he knew that underneath it all, he had as black a heart as anyone. This way he was entertaining as he tried to put on airs and was hilarious when he ran in sheer panic from the crocodile. It was a complicated personality to discover as the crew worked on the storyboards and wrote dialogue, and we were

insidious planning showed he was thinking and the thought process is the animator's way of giving life to the character. He was convincingly alive when he was trying to trick Tinker Bell into revealing information about Peter Pan. The high point came when he became aggravated with her delays, exploded, then

Captain Hook's frustration causes him to momentarily explode as Tinker Bell stops walking and turns to ask a question. But he quickly regains his composure. Animation by Frank Thomas.

caught himself quickly and said, "Continue, my dear," in his most ingratiating manner. It was important to show this side of Hook's personality in order to make the marvelous slapstick scenes ring true. Farce is always based on sincerity and believability.

Mr. Smee was the comic sidekick who agreed with Captain Hook's philosophy but lacked the intelligence and physical stature to carry out any really villainous plan. He was always there for Hook to play to, to explain things to and to display the subtleties of personality that made the captain such an interesting villain. Mr. Smee did not understand what was going on most of the time, but in his own way he certainly had villainy in his heart.

Author and historian John Culhane pointed out the innate corruption in Mr. Smee's personality when he assisted Captain Hook in leaving the "beautiful little Indian maiden, Tiger Lily, bound in the water until she either betrays the location of Peter's hideout or drowns in the incoming tide. Smee is the perfect picture of the banality of evil: a short, fat, balding, blundering, nearsighted fool with the I.Q. of a turnip who is 'only following orders,' and seems to have dehumanized the Indian child out of his lack of imagination so that he doesn't even realize that he may be helping to kill an innocent child."

The crocodile was villainous only as far as

Captain Hook was concerned. He was no threat to anyone else in the cast, which helped make his intended victim even more special. Because of his sheer size and history of having eaten the captain's hand at an earlier time, he was believable and taken seriously, yet all his actions were comic and usually a bit preposterous. There was no doubt that he intended to eat as much of Captain Hook as he could. Captain Hook never doubted it and neither did the audience. Once that had been established, there was no limit to what the crocodile could do in order to enrich a situation. He was responsible for some of the best comedy we ever achieved in feature production.

111

Walt had told us, "Instead of killing anybody we ought to get rid of them. . . . Maybe with the crocodile and Hook —the crocodile is waiting for him—then have a funny chase— the last you see is Hook going like hell. That's better than having him get caught . . . the audience will get to liking Hook and they won't want to see him killed."

Mr. Smee is a caricature of a blundering, stupid pirate who tries to follow Captain Hook's orders whether he understands them or not.

Tiger Lily will be left to drown inside Skull Rock unless she gives Hook the information he seeks.

Aunt Sarah and her cats made life very difficult for Lady but there was no scheming or treachery, except for the natural reaction of cats to a dog that is trying to protect her house.

Lady and the Tramp

There is no true villain in this romantic and nostalgic story, only desperate and difficult situations as one character confronts another. Aunt Sarah is not trying to be mean. She just likes cats better than dogs, and her responsibility here is to take care of the baby. Through the unfortunate accidents that occur, as well as those caused by her Siamese cats, Aunt Sarah believes that Lady is a threat to the baby and must be muzzled, and later removed. There is no malice in either action; it is just good common sense. She is not psychopathic, or a villainess, or a crusader out to rid the world of dogs. She is totally unaware that any of her actions are affecting the lives of our canine cast. The dogs, of course, are unable to do anything except run away, which Lady would never do. Tramp has the more difficult situation of being turned over to the dogcatcher, and certain death, and without voices to explain or argue or plead, they are both helpless. In many ways, the bold, insensitive zealot is as much of a problem as an evil, scheming monster.

The Siamese cats are funny because everyone who has ever owned one has endless stories of their strange, unexpected behavior, completely self-centered (as are all cats), with aggressive personalities. There is nothing you can do with them, or about them, for that matter. Their antics in this film to discredit Lady and get her out of the house are so close to reality that the cats cannot really be blamed for what they do. Bad as it is, it is still only the "naughtiness" that we have come to expect from them.

The Rat is all animal. In the early story work, he was a sly personality with comic overtones. But for the danger and threat he posed to the baby, and the integrity that would be needed for his fight with Tramp, it seemed better to have him a "real" rat. The animator who was cast on this sequence, Wolfgang "Woolie" Reitherman, wanted to capture the movements of the real animal, so he had the carpenter shop build a large cage that could fit into his room next to his desk, and he filled it with over a dozen rats. He had been frustrated a few years earlier by his assignment to animate dinosaurs for *Fantasia* with no model to stimulate his imagination. Now he wanted to observe day after day until he had the feel of an animal, how it moved, how it reacted, how it thought.

For several weeks before he began animating he watched his new roommates, mostly out of the corner of his eye while he was completing another assignment. At first he had many curious visitors who could not believe that anyone could subject themselves to such a study, but as the smell increased, the novelty wore off and soon he was alone with the rats nearly all of each day. The animation he eventually created was just what the picture needed,

That was the giant challenge to the staff and especially to the Nine Old Men, as Walt gradually spent more time on his other interests. His hobbies of a few years earlier had now become full-scale, exciting realities. Year by year, as he was happily planning Disneyland, the TV shows, the Mickey Mouse Club and the live-action films, the control of the animated films was turned over to the staff more than we had ever expected or wanted. It was much more comfortable for us to implement Walt's ideas on the screen than facing the uncertainty of animating a section of our own that did not feel as strong or as entertaining as we wanted. We made up for our weaknesses with rich characters and acting and we all agreed that the most important parts were the villains and their victims.

the rat the perfect adversary for Tramp, believable and formidable, with the quickness and danger of the living animal.

This gave Tramp the chance to show his true colors, to be the hero as well as the brash individualist who got Lady into trouble. It could easily have been sentimental and essentially theatrical, but with this special animation, the fight with the rat provided the strength that the story needed for everything else to play out convincingly.

Walt in one meeting had told of a famous story about a pioneer returning to his cabin to find that his dog had torn up the place. He whipped the poor animal to make sure it learned its lesson, then as he started picking up the clothes and bedding, he discovered the body of a freshly killed rattlesnake. The faithful dog had risked his own life to protect his master. Walt wanted the same intensity of emotions in the fight between Tramp and the Rat, and after outlining his thoughts on the continuity, he left the mechanics and techniques to us.

A cartoon rat was considered at one time but when the dogs became so believable, the idea was dropped. That decision forced the animator to make the rat as realistic as he could.

ZIP!

The rat was the only really villainous character and yet even he was only following his natural instincts. It is not always necessary to have a true villain around in order to have serious problems in one's life.

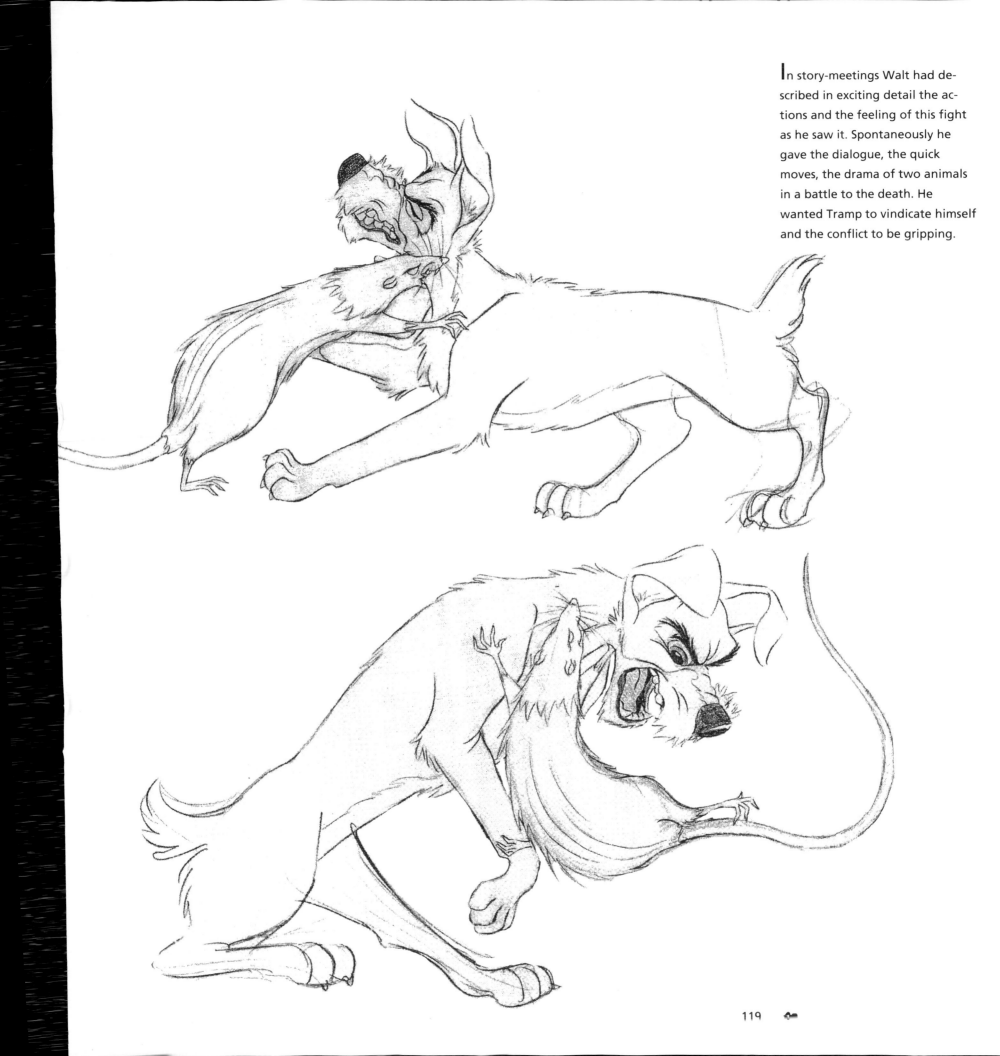

In story-meetings Walt had described in exciting detail the actions and the feeling of this fight as he saw it. Spontaneously he gave the dialogue, the quick moves, the drama of two animals in a battle to the death. He wanted Tramp to vindicate himself and the conflict to be gripping.

Maleficent relies on her faithful raven to search the whole kingdom for any sign of the Princess Aurora. Her location is discovered by the sight of colorful magic dust escaping up the chimney of a cottage.

Story sketches show the fateful moment when the hypnotized Aurora touches the spindle of the spinning wheel at Maleficent's command.

Maleficent has strong magic and mythical powers.

As long as Prince Phillip is Maleficent's prisoner Aurora will never be awakened from her sleep. The final animation drawing (left) from the scene, and as it appeared on the screen (right) all inked and painted and with a background.

substantial combination, she easily dominated every scene. Her aloofness and treachery made it difficult for the audience to understand her motives much of the time. No one ever knew if the trouble at the christening was caused by her anger at not being invited or some form of jealousy toward those who were. However, she was so domineering in both attitude and design that no one even thought of questioning what she was doing. Who would dare argue with Maleficent?

Because of this icy reserve, her relationship with Aurora became shadowy since the girl was always isolated from the great threat she was under. She never knew through the whole picture what all the precautions were for. Even when she climbed the stairs to the spinning wheel at the castle, she was hypnotized and not aware of what was happening. A few of us wondered if she would have been a more interesting character if she had come face to face with Maleficent and had somehow been forced against her will to prick her finger and die. Walt disagreed, feeling that this eerie, haunting presentation of a victim powerless in the hands of evil was the strongest and best statement for the film. At the end, it placed more of a burden on the prince to overcome such a force in order to save Aurora.

Prince Phillip was actually more of a victim than Aurora, which gave us a hero who had reason to fight back, both to get himself

The goons celebrate the capture of Prince Phillip, under the watchful eye of Maleficent.

out of Maleficent's clutches and to rescue his loved one as well. By default, the three Good Fairies had also become surrogate victims, and even though they were not personally vulnerable, their combined powers could not match Maleficent's magic and they had to rely on the little help they could give the prince in order to win the sympathy of the audience.

The raven was an extension of Maleficent's sinister personality but portrayed in a more active way. With all the magic at her command, it was slightly surprising that the Evil Fairy had to rely on the spying activities of her raven to gain the crucial knowledge of the girl's whereabouts. Yet there was more impact in his seeing the telltale evidence in the pink and blue magic dust than if Maleficent had discovered it in some kind of crystal ball. This way, the fallibility of the Good Fairies played an important role in causing their plan to fail. That is easier for the audience to relate to and understand than some kind of magical radar.

The designs for Maleficent's squadron of vile, little helpers, the goons, were first based on the gargoyles and subordinate devils of that same Gothic period. As their role in the film developed, they gradually became more of a twentieth-century artist's fantasy. Finally it was determined that they could be comical in their stupidity to lighten the brooding heaviness of Maleficent's domain. There was something rather unexpected in her having such irresponsible workers to defend her impregnable castle, but it probably made her slightly more vulnerable and the ending more believable.

Dramatic action, color, design and animation all came together when Maleficent became the dragon in a last attempt to defeat Prince Phillip. Instead of becoming a

new personality to match her frightening reptilian form, she was still the familiar Maleficent, only now apparently invincible. Her dragon's eyes had no pupils, which suggested that you were looking across the lids into some kind of inferno as you did in viewing Chernobog. There was an eerie sensation and a scary feeling in looking into the eyes of such a beast.

Powerful and dazzling, the battle was one of the most startling and vivid to be conceived in animated films. It left the audience with such a lasting impression of visual excitement that they scarcely remembered the earlier weaker moments. The overall beauty of the picture gave the impression that we had equaled the care for detail and extra expense that had been present in the Golden Age.

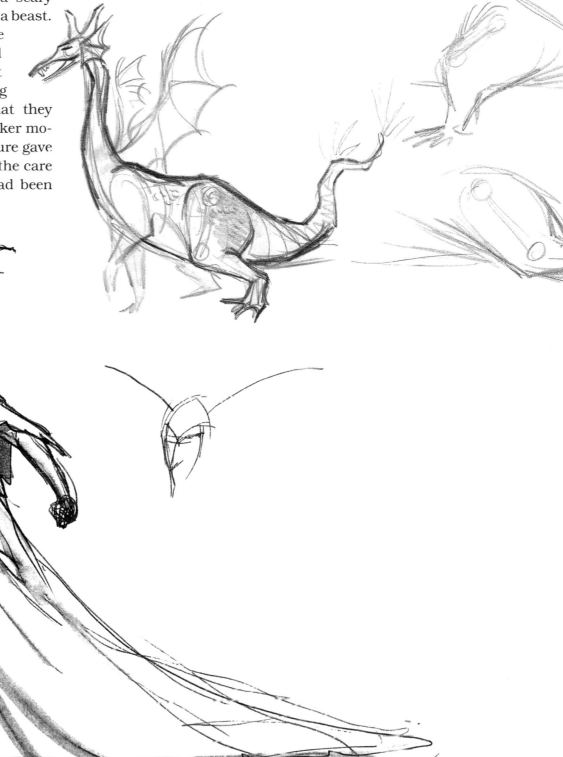

Many suggestions are tried in shape, design, and detail before a final model is approved. Early ideas for both the dragon and Maleficent.

In the original story by Dodie Smith, Cruella was presented as a spoiled, blasé, inconsiderate daughter of a wealthy family. The studio's concept was considerably more flamboyant, dangerous, and humorous.

"I don't like her much," said Cruella. "I'd drown her if she wasn't so valuable."

The household's joy over the birth of Perdita's puppies is shattered as Cruella interrupts to complain about the lack of spots on the newborn.

Cruella shows her wild, bizarre side even when she's happy.

101 Dalmatians

By the time *Sleeping Beauty* was completed in 1959, the storymen and the directors' units were experienced and better trained to take on the additional responsibilities. The first of their villains was Cruella De Vil in *101 Dalmatians*, who was diabolical but not a schemer; she never thought anything over, reacting instead in purely emotional ways. The author of the original story, Dodie Smith, had created the basic character; our top storyman, Bill Peet, had developed the erratic behavior and added the comic touch to each macabre situation; and conceptual artist Ken Anderson had contributed style, design and additional situations.

Still, Cruella required even greater flair to be as sensational as the picture needed. It came from the outstanding voice of Betty Lou Gerson, who was intimidating even to the other actresses working with her; the live-action stimulation of Mary Wickes, who showed the possibilities in rawboned angularity as against a slick, sophisticated smoothness; and the spirited animation of Marc Davis, who was not sure his comic interpretation fit with the other human characters. With

this crew behind her, Cruella suddenly sprang to life in a way that was both humorous and threatening.

Betty Lou Gerson said, "Cruella is a very interesting character. She's the only villainess who doesn't use magic; she's a dirty, mean dame but everyone can relate to her. She's real." Cruella was certainly real. She had an abrasive personality, a terrible temper, outlandish taste, and was cruel without concern or remorse. She was also selfish and spoiled, and completely lacking in self-control. She blew up at Roger and Anita because she couldn't have the puppies. She wrecked her expensive car rather than allow the truck with

Horace and Jasper Badun have been hired to take care of the ninety-nine Dalmatian puppies they have kidnapped.

Cruella watches intently as a long row of black puppies crosses in front of her car. She is suspicious but would never consider that these dogs could be her intended victims.

The cat, Sergeant
Tibbs, has brought
Pongo and Perdita
out to rescue the
pups and take them
back to London.

Cruella gives chase in her expensive car, but is suddenly pushed off the road by the Baduns in a small van of their own. Excellent story sketches by Bill Peet give the feeling of excitement and activity on a cold winter day.

the stowaway puppies to get back to London. Everything is out in the open with her. The victims are aware that they are in great danger but don't know what to do about it or how to avoid it. There is no secret about this villain's plans and she will not be denied in getting what she wants. This brings out the heroism of Pongo and Perdita and all the animals in the area who so willingly offer their help.

Her henchmen, Horace and Jasper Badun, were small-time crooks, mean and argumentative, who caused Cruella problems that revealed the depth of her psychosis. In a way, they brought out the best in her, since she was funniest when her frustrations boiled over. On their own, the Baduns would probably have limited their illegal pursuits to common skulduggery and theft. As crooks for hire, they could be talked into doing any job Cruella's warped mind would conceive, which made them considerably more dangerous. It was a sparkling combination of unnerving evil intent and ridiculous farce, played against the innocence and vulnerability of ninety-nine puppies. Few actresses ever have an opportunity to play such a role. Cruella was unique, outrageous and highly entertaining. She was one of our most popular villains.

A sad Perdita knows that Cruella will somehow get her puppies once they are born.

An early story sketch suggests that both Pongo and Perdita stand guard over their offspring as Cruella extends a gloved hand for them.

The Sword in the Stone

The Sword in the Stone (1963), based on the book by T. H. White, was made up of many incidents that helped the young King Arthur prepare for his later role in history, and did not have a plot motivated by any real villain. Arthur, who was called Wart at the time, was being tutored by the legendary Merlin, and together they participated in several dangerous adventures around the castle of Sir Ector. Still the most entertaining and innovative section was the one that featured the Mad Madam Mim, Merlin's defiant adversary, who had captured the boy and was about to destroy him because he represented good. As she said, "In my book, that's bad!" She believed that she was the world's most powerful wizard and nearly proved it in the spirited competition with Merlin called the Wizards' Duel.

Mim was first seen cheating at solitaire, which for her was as moral and honorable an attitude as we ever saw. She could transform herself into anything, never played fair, was an out-and-out liar and was naturally a poor loser. With the voice of Martha Wentworth, she was a cross between an aging spoiled brat and a young crotchety hag. She was a great character, being alive and vibrant and fun to animate, but the story was not constructed to use her in more than one cameo appearance.

Sir Ector, Wart's foster father, was another in our group of unkind persons who lacked imagination and understanding. He was autocratic, made snap judgments and knew exactly how he wanted things to be in his domain, but he was not a simpleton, and in time usually recognized the wisdom of Merlin's ideas.

The big oaf, Kay, was surly and a bully and caused problems for Wart throughout the picture, but he was a dolt. A bigger threat was in his example of what Wart's life would be like if he remained a peasant on Sir Ector's farm. There was no happiness in Kay, only the crudeness of a dull-witted ego.

The large pike in the moat who almost caught Wart when he was a fish and the scrawny wolf who always followed him in the woods were stereotyped comic fare, providing both pressure and laughs without a distinct personality in either category. Many times it is more important for the villain to be only credible, with the needs of the story coming first.

The differences in philosophy between Merlin and Madam Mim are evident just in their body attitudes as they march off to begin the Wizards' Duel.

Madam Mim as a pretty girl with purple hair, talking to a sparrow, who is really Wart, and (bottom) she changes back to herself once more.

Mim feigns sympathy as she tells Wart that she must destroy him.

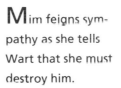

Madam Mim (top) thinks on what she wants to change herself into; (middle) she pulls her hair down over her face, and (bottom) reveals her choice, an ugly old hag. She is happy about her prowess.

Bill Peet drew the whole story in sketches like these, developing each character and each bit of acting; (top) closeup of the "pretty girl" being sweet to Wart as a sparrow; (middle) the unfortunate wolf who never gets a bite of Wart, and (bottom) the dull-witted Kay, son of Sir Ector, foster father to Wart.

Ken Anderson suggested how the interior of Madam Mim's house might look. Ken was especially helpful in showing the props a character would own.

Walt had expressly asked us not to create another slavering, menacing tiger. In a TV presentation of Hemingway's short story, *The Killers*, the handling of the villains showed them to be so tough, so cruel, so self-assured that they did not need to threaten. Their very self-confidence was terrifying. This gave us a new idea.

The Jungle Book

The Jungle Book (1967) was another picture based on a series of incidents with vignettes of new characters and varied personalities rather than a complete story line. Essentially, it was a travelogue of the adventures of the boy Mowgli on his journey from the jungle where he had been raised by wolves to the safety of the "manvillage." Few of the animals he met along the way had any sympathy for his predicament and several were genuinely hostile. The leader of the elephant brigade, a stuffy and pompous old colonel left over from British colonial days, wanted Mowgli completely out of the jungle. His crustiness was balanced by the sympathetic attitude of his wife and that of his young son, who was briefly a playmate for the boy.

King Louie, the orangutan ruler of the monkeys, wanted to know how to make fire and captured Mowgli in hopes of finding out the secret. We had thought of this ape as being surly, morose, possibly abusive

Colonel Hathi, the leader of the elephant brigade, threatens Mowgli, "I'll have no mancub in my jungle!"

and impossible to talk to. As the sequence developed, it seemed better to have a musical section with a jungle beat and a "swinging" king who was still after something he wanted but was easily distracted by the rhythm of the monkeys' music. Louis Prima was chosen for the voice and immediately we had a wonderful, new character. As an animal, King Louie was low in mentality, unpredictable and concerned only with his own wishes. As a personality, he was sparkling, happy and rhythmic in both his movements and his dialogue. This created a toe-tapping type of suspense that was enjoyable to us as animators and to the audiences everywhere. Prima became so emotionally involved in the creation of his animated counterpart that he regularly called the Disney animation staff from Lake Tahoe, where he was performing with his

K_{aa}, the overconfident python, enjoys his sly ways of
capturing a victim: assumed innocence, smooth, comfort-
ing manner, and a big show of compassion for the problems of his prey.

Kaa hypnotizes the boy in preparation for a nice meal. Story sketches by Vance Gerry.

Kaa will not give up his long-anticipated dinner.

Kaa has been pushed out of the tree by Mowgli, who now accuses Kaa of lying.

The young and foolish Mowgli has neither fear nor respect for the mighty tiger. This boy will grow into a very wise young man—if he survives.

band, to offer his thoughts on character and plot development. He even wanted King Louie to be killed because he knew he could do such a wonderful death scene.

More sinister, but just as entertaining, was the mighty python, Kaa. His big problem was that he could not keep his mouth shut when he needed to be quiet. He was so proud of his abilities, his slyness, his superior ways that he negated many nearly successful ventures before they were quite consummated. The first night, Mowgli and Bagheera, his companion-protector, had climbed into the branches of a tall tree, only to have Kaa slither down beside them and quickly wrap the boy up for a late-evening snack. When the tired Bagheera heard the mumbling he had said, "No more talk until morning." Kaa could not restrain himself from replying, "He won't be here in the morning." He lost two chances for meals that night and was humiliated in the bargain.

Our first attempts at casting for a voice

unearthed much sibilance but not enough personality. Then someone suggested Sterling Holloway, who had done many voices for us in the past, mainly for mice. He projected an innocence and lack of strength as to be almost asexual, which was ideal for our snake. He was definitely a new type of villain, enthusiastic and overconfident in his anticipation of success and petulant in his failures.

Kaa and Mowgli met a second time when the boy was more concerned with his feelings of rejection than with escaping from a real killer. He was easily hypnotized while Kaa sang "Trust in me, just in me . . ." It would have been possible to make this encounter a thrilling episode if we had played it from Mowgli's standpoint with the suspense and danger in facing the mighty python and the futility of his attempted defense. But there was more entertainment in seeing how Kaa subdued his prey, especially when it was a brash youngster who refused to recognize the seriousness of his situation. This way the tension came a little later when the tiger, Shere Khan, visited Kaa, and the two opponents were more evenly matched.

Shere Khan was one of our most interesting villains. He was physically strong, agile and capable, but did not have a "tough guy" attitude. There was no need for a swagger, no show-off, no having to prove himself. The storyman, Bill Peet, had drawn a powerful, mean character, aloof and cold. Ken Anderson had added arrogance and a Basil Rathbone touch of intelligence and culture. He was above the other animals of the jungle. Like a Roman emperor or a medieval king, he accepted complete authority as his due; there was no need to wallow in the glory of his position. Unlike those monarchs, he did not have to worry about assassins or treachery in the ranks.

The perfect choice for the voice was George Sanders, the complete cynic, who added the element of boredom. With this voice, we could imagine a tiger who would kill without concern or effort. Sanders was asked if he would like a drawing of Shere Khan as a souvenir, to which he responded, "I suppose so." Asked further if he would like Walt to autograph it, he replied, "How utterly absurd. Why would I want his signature? He might want mine; I created the character."

Of course, that view was not shared by Milt Kahl, who was one of the finest draftsmen at the studio, a top animator and the artist who brought this tiger to life. Milt had the self-confidence of his animated offspring and the intelligence as well. With his skills, Shere Khan finally became a complete personality, smooth, handsome, egotistical and convincing.

It is not often that true villains as unique as Kaa and Shere Khan confront each other. In *The Jungle Book* the meeting was not a victim-villain relationship because they had nearly equal strengths. It was more a game of "keep away." Kaa will not admit that he has Mowgli hypnotized high in the tree as the tiger suspects. In a cold but polite manner Shere Khan tries to intimidate the crafty Kaa by suggesting, "I thought you might be entertaining someone up there in your coils."

He has Kaa by the throat, but the snake is willing to gamble that he can talk his way out of this situation. Looking very innocent, he answers, "Coils? Someone? Oh — I was just curling up for my s-s-siesta."

Shere Khan holds a long, sharp claw to the snake's throat.

"But you were singing to someone. Who is it, Kaa?"

"Oh, I was just — ah — singing — ah — to myself."

"Indeed," replies Shere Khan.

The tiger is almost unbeatable, but he is unable to find out if Mowgli is really up in the tree. Any other character would have been terrified by the treatment Kaa is receiving, yet the snake continues to be evasive. He is a slippery antagonist, withstanding threats and humiliation in order to keep Mowgli for himself. It is an entertaining standoff for these two powerful predators, but it is Mowgli who eventually wins the day.

Walt never saw the finished film. It had been the last time he worked with us and suddenly there was a great void where his guidance and support had always been. Even though we had been weaned from most of his influence, his death in December 1966 was a shattering loss to all of us. Ironically, the success of *The Jungle Book* brought a renewed interest in animation, and as young artists submitted applications, the training program was revived and the future of villains and victims, heroes and comedians, was once more assured.

The Aristocats

Four more features were produced before retirements cut deeply into our ranks. *The Aristocats,* a story about an elderly woman and her beloved family of cats who were to inherit her fortune, had intrigued Walt but he had not had time to have a meeting with any of the staff who would be making the film. The villain, who was not outstanding as a character but was needed by the story line, was the butler in the household, who was to inherit Madame's fortune *after* the cats. This was more than he could accept and he tried des- perately to get rid of the felines, who were destined to have control of this money for at least another fifteen years. It was decided to make him a comic character rather than a heavy villain, forgoing suspense for humor and diabolical craftiness for bungling.

Fortunately, the success of the picture did not rely on any deep villain-victim relation- ship and the other incidents and characters furnished the main entertainment. A sinister butler would probably have been out of place, since the cat family's plight was more incon- venient than perilous.

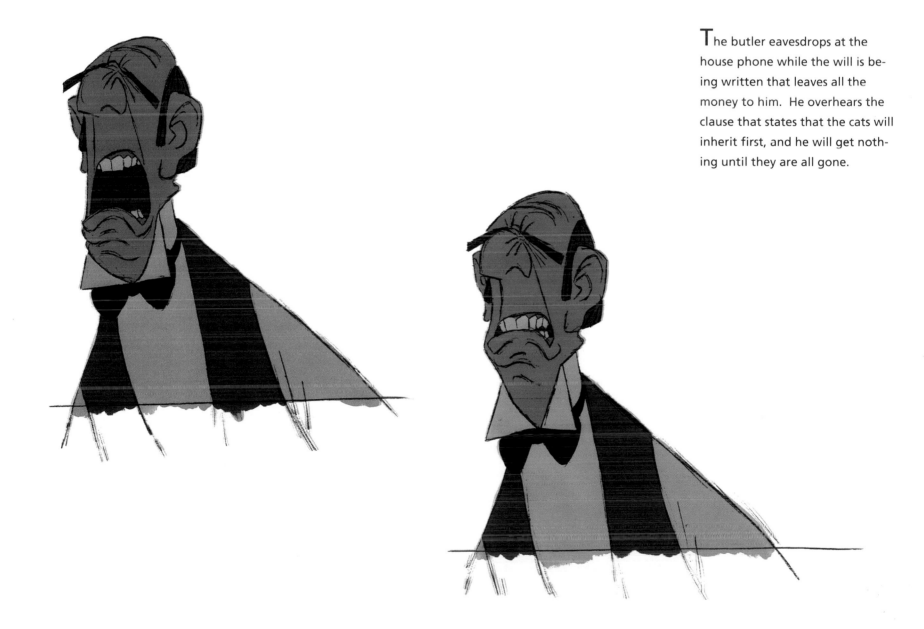

The butler eavesdrops at the house phone while the will is be- ing written that leaves all the money to him. He overhears the clause that states that the cats will inherit first, and he will get noth- ing until they are all gone.

His despair leads him to ominous thoughts of getting rid of the cats.

The butler tries to ship the cats far, far away in a trunk.

Duchess, the mother cat, with one of her kittens. The family faces an uncertain future.

Robin Hood

Robin Hood (1973) was planned as a light-hearted musical with three scruffy villains and an invincible hero. None of us wanted a heavy, dramatic, believable adventure, but we felt that the villains should be nasty and formidable in order to properly challenge Robin's talents. Ken Anderson started us off with a series of sketches of each character with suggestions for their personalities. The snake, Sir Hiss, was menacing and sneaky, slipping into places where he could eavesdrop and take back news to Prince John. Others in the cast never knew where he was or if it was safe to talk since he could be anywhere. Ken drew many sketches of his long, narrow body hidden under furniture, in a suit of armor, even a potted plant.

The Sheriff of Nottingham was physically strong, suspicious of everyone and very alert. In his job as tax collector, he constantly moved around the community, observing everything that was going on. He was feared by all, for it was known that if he dragged you in, you never came out. No one argued with this guy!

Prince John was neurotic and unpredictable; he had disposed of his brother, King Richard, so now the throne was his, but he would have a hard time holding it. He was obsessed with getting rid of Robin Hood and tried constantly to achieve that goal.

As the whole unit worked on the story concept we gradually realized that these three were all essentially alike. Three mean, squinty-eyed, capable villains increased Robin Hood's problems but they also made problems for the story crew in finding entertainment in the situations. A change was needed and the three outstanding actors who were providing the voices of our three villains, Peter Ustinov as Prince John, Pat Buttram as the Sheriff and Terry-Thomas as Sir Hiss, were asked to contribute their ideas. Each of these talented

The Prince of many moods reveals his inner feelings. Story sketches by Vance Gerry, Ken Anderson and Al Wilson.

Suspicious

Scheming

Humble

Dissatisfied

Satisfied

Angry

performers could build personality traits and write dialogue to fit, so working together, we were able to make the characters lighter and richer, with better comic possibilities.

Terry-Thomas gave us a snake that was much less formidable and even had a touch of pathos. With a soft, insinuating voice and an ingratiating manner, he was the complete sycophant. In spite of his high office, no one respected or feared him because they knew that Prince John had no respect for him either. There was no other place he could go or position that he could hold. His only life was with Prince John and that was a miserable life. He was hit, maligned, ignored and blamed for nearly everything. He was no longer sinister, although he tried to be. Most of all, Sir Hiss wanted to be important. He was smarter than both Prince John and the Sheriff, but it did him no good. He was rather pathetic, and ludicrous.

Pat Buttram, the all-round comic, gave

Mother!

It's not fair!

Getting the idea

To heck with them — I'm still king.

Selling the idea

What went wrong this time?

Oh, no-o-o!

The Sheriff of Nottingham collects the taxes from the poor.

The Sheriff watches over the jail with the help of Trigger and Nutsy, his two trusted guards.

Sir Hiss uses various disguises to spy on the crowd.

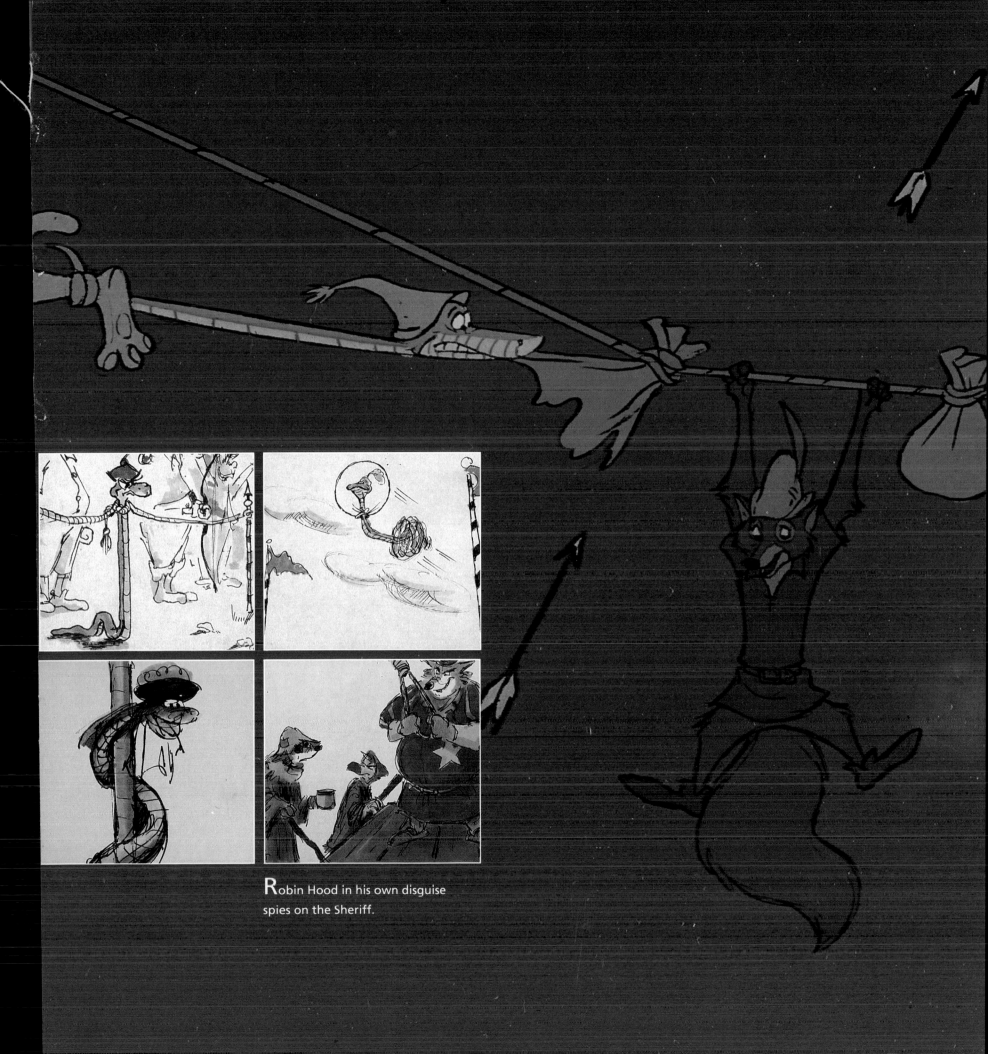

Robin Hood in his own disguise spies on the Sheriff.

Prince John has captured Robin
Hood at the tournament, but the
wily fox will escape once more with
the help of his friends.

Sir Hiss realizes too late
that he has said some-
thing wrong again.

his Sheriff new lines and attitudes, retaining the crafty and suspicious nature but reducing his mental powers considerably. This lawman was conceited, enjoyed being mean and used his position to intimidate the populace. He was happy with what he had. His boss liked him and he believed that he alone knew what Robin Hood would do in any situation. He was formidable because of his powerful rank, which was enforced by his two buzzard deputies, Trigger and Nutsy. These misfits were overly eager to enforce law and order whether it was needed or not. In their attempts to be supportive, they usually contradicted what the Sheriff was trying to do and created worse situations for everyone but Robin Hood.

The incomparable actor Peter Ustinov created a completely new Prince John who was even more neurotic, but dangerous because he was the ruler and not bright enough for the job. Vain and childish, he was easily duped, yet still retained his delusions of being a terrific monarch, clever enough to rid himself forever of Robin Hood. He kept thinking up elaborate traps to catch this outlaw, then blamed the snake for their failures. Both Prince John and Sir Hiss were worried that history would pass them by, that they really didn't matter. They were both trying desperately to make their mark, to be remembered. Many real villains are driven by this need to be noticed, to make a difference in other people's lives.

The biggest problem in the picture was that Robin Hood was intrinsically invincible. No matter what anyone did, he was always in control, always winning. Prince John was incompetent, insecure, trying to live someone else's life — his brother's. He was only a menace when he had ample backing, but since no one could get the better of Robin Hood in the first place, it did not make much difference. Sir Hiss saw through situations more quickly than Prince John, which made an entertaining relationship for them, but it could not help the story itself.

In this film, the villains were actually the victims, and the supposed victim was a classic hero. With the usual roles reversed, the villains were funny, while Robin Hood was the mastermind, the capable instigator — he acted and the villains reacted. They offered the danger of the situations, but the popularity of the legend was all based on making the villains look ridiculous. Try as we could, Robin Hood never seemed to be in any danger, really.

Medusa uses her powerful personality instead of magic to control those around her, including these two crocodile guardians.

The Rescuers

In one of Margery Sharp's books about Bernard and Bianca, the two resolute mice from the Rescue Aid Society, there was an appealing story of a little girl who was held captive by a very cold, cruel elderly woman. The plot offered drama and suspense but not much humor. Those of us planning the production decided to make our villain a much more flashy, eccentric personality. The film was released in 1977 and was called *The Rescuers*.

A clear and strong victim-villain relationship was the basis for this story about a five-year-old girl, Penny, and her two mice rescuers, up against a flamboyant criminal, Medusa, and a pair of crocodiles. The largest diamond in the world had been buried in a cave along the coast by pirates years before, and now Medusa had kidnapped Penny from an orphanage to aid in the life-threatening endeavor to retrieve it.

We worked and reworked our story to understand this woman's consuming desire and her ominous plans, but most of all we needed a special voice that would bring her to life. We found it in Geraldine Page. From her first line, we knew we had possibly the greatest voice for animation we had ever had. Suddenly, the character was there before us, alive, vain and fanatical. Surpassing any of the timid concepts we had worked with so

The crocodiles search for the escaped girl around the boat while Medusa shines her flashlight along the shore line.

Ken also suggested some business of the mice hiding in an old organ and the crocs trying to blow them out where they could be caught.

arduously before, this Medusa was overwhelming, authoritative and entertaining. An animator had little to do other than follow her lead to establish an outstanding villain. Fortunately, the animator, Milt Kahl, went far beyond that, knowing that this would be his last picture for the studio before his retirement. He wanted to go out with a creation that would stand without equal.

While that is a very exciting aim, from a practical standpoint, it is difficult to judge when one is doing his best work. It is so easy to be swayed by small successes and lose perspective on the needs of the overall picture. As much as we think we know filmmaking and character development and theories of villain-victim relationships, in order to have a memorable performance there always has to be a touch of magic in the production process that goes beyond any single individual. The proper chemistry between staff members is essential and some combination of talent and experience is necessary, but nothing can quite match that extra element of "fairy dust" in creating a masterpiece.

First of all, Medusa was a drawing. The audience was not asked to believe that she was real. Like Cruella, she was a caricature of a wild type of female.

While we played with story ideas and interesting situations with the mice from the Rescue Aid Society, Ken Anderson started drawing different types of strange women, from old maid school teachers, to women's clubs chairpersons, to sloppy, insensitive dames, to petty crime perpetrators. For a while we considered using Cruella De Vil again, but preferred not to make a sequel to any of our pictures.

159

Medusa holds Penny's teddy bear hostage as she puts the girl down the hole into the cave. Penny searches for the world's largest diamond which is hidden down there. Medusa clutches the diamond, forgetting about Penny's safety or Mr. Snoops's part interest in their venture.

larger than life, ridiculous in many ways, but always fascinating. Then, somehow, a touch of silliness crept into the interpretation that kept her from being our strongest villain. When there was a choice between a humorous way to act as opposed to a sinister one, the comic version always won out. Charles Champlin, emeritus fine arts editor of the *Los Angeles Times*, had commented that she looked more like a frowzy, over-the-hill nightclub singer than an intimidating villain. Of course, literature is full of soft and pudgy women who are absorbed with evil thoughts, so that should not have mattered.

Whatever the problem, Medusa ended up being slightly less convincing and having less intensity and drive in her acting than Cruella. Charles Solomon, current animation critic for the *Los Angeles Times*, thought she did not have the kind of situations to play out that Ursula or Cruella had. "And she's so excited about the diamond, she ceases to be menacing. She wants the diamond, the wonderful diamond, the huge diamond — she's being more comic than she needs to be."

A few of us wondered if Medusa would deliberately kill anyone. She was completely self-centered, irresponsible and prone to moments of panic when she went utterly insane. She blasted the mice with her shotgun and peppered Mr. Snoops with some wild shots, but you could predict that she was going to miss and destroy only her furniture. Somehow, after she fell off the chair while trying to get away from the mouse, she lost her strength as a potential killer. She was still a definite threat because she could have forgotten about Penny and left her in the cave to drown, or shot at someone in a fit of anger and hit the mark, or accidentally run over someone in her swampmobile while trying to stop the escape and the ensuing loss of her diamond. Killing was not a part of her villainy.

The elements in the cave were the real menace, because they were mechanical, predictable and relentless. The rising of the tide did not depend on an unstable mind and its whims. It was Nature, mindlessly carrying

Preliminary sketches show the attempts to find the right attitude for Medusa leaping up on a chair to escape the mice. Mr. Snoops rushes to the rescue with a broom, but succeeds only in knocking the chair out from under her. With this fall, Medusa gets a laugh but loses her strength as a real villain; she is still dangerous and can cause trouble for everyone, but she is no longer the driving force of the picture.

out the routine events of the day. Placing the young girl in such a threatening situation was the extent of Medusa's fiendish plan.

At the studio, we all loved this enthralling caricature of a wicked individual, but somehow she was less memorable with the audiences. It might have been some weakness in the story construction, or a lack of believability in her acting, or the fact that most of the attempts to be funny had softened her potential. Possibly there was some confusion over what her role was supposed to do for the story. Her love for her pet crocodiles and her total disdain for her assistant, Mr. Snoops, gave unexpected dimension to her personality; the drawing was great, the animation imaginative, the voice terrific. To us, she was undeniably one of our great villains. Still, many people feel that the magnificent tiger, Shere Khan, is Milt's greatest contribution to our group of evil characters.

Author John Culhane had asked Milt Kahl to speak to his students at the School of Visual Arts in New York. Milt was also asked to make a drawing for a poster to advertise the event, so he drew a caricature of himself with Robin Hood, who he was animating at the time, and showing Culhane as a ventriloquist's dummy on his knee. When Milt showed the poster to Woolie Reitherman, John Culhane reports, "Woolie pointed at the caricature of me and said, 'There's our villain for *The Rescuers*, Medusa's sidekick — Mr. Snoops!'" John continued, "Becoming a Disney character was beyond my wildest dreams of glory."

John Culhane claims he was tricked into posing for various attitudes, which like this one, ended up on the Mr. Snoops model sheet. The voice was furnished by Joe Flynn, but the action was all based on John.

The Fox and the Hound

The film that marked the final transition from the old timers to the new trainees who were eager to try out some of their own ideas was *The Fox and the Hound.* It was another story with confronting characters in strong situations but no real villains. It was mainly about two natural enemies who had been friends and playmates when they were young and the deterioration of this friendship as they grew to maturity. The dog, Copper, was raised to be a hunter, and the fox, Tod, was programmed by instinct to raid the henhouse and tease the dogs. Inevitably there was a misunderstanding and the dog became an outspoken enemy of his former friend.

The hunter was more concerned with making a living off the furs he could sell than maliciously trying to get even with this particular fox. The bear who became the common danger for both Copper and Tod was the only creature who was vicious and determined enough to kill, but this was just a wild animal's reaction to the attack. So who was the villain? Everybody? Or no one?

The young animator, Glen Keane, who was handling this section thought there should be much more excitement in that final fight with the enraged bear and his combatants, who were fast becoming his victims.

As in the battle between the Tyrannosaurus Rex and the Stegosaurus in *Fantasia*, Glen wanted an awesome conflict devoid of villainy or personality that built on raw power and dynamic visuals. He asked if he could take the sequence and sketch up some new continuity that would add danger and tempo and drama. He added swirling mist from a waterfall, savage scenes of brute force for the bear, strength and darting moves for the fox and the hound. It was a thrilling climax to the picture and set up the emotional impact of the rebirth of friendship between the two animals. Glen's concept went far beyond the ordinary story sketches that he had been given, and established him as a top directing animator for the new era.

All the new animators still faced several frustrating years as they gained experience and confidence. With Walt gone and those of us he had trained no longer available, it was

The fox is no match for the ferocious bear, but he cannot give up.

difficult to grasp the full importance of the values that had guided our work and they began to seek out a new style that was right for them. Generally they felt that *Snow White and the Seven Dwarfs* was an old-fashioned love story full of great songs. It was wonderful, but the tempo was slow. They wanted either sophisticated farce or more vigor and energy in both the music they would use and the pictures they would make. They were interested in characters with real depth, everyday personalities caught up in conflicts of desires and difficult resolutions. Rather than the single-minded villains of forty years earlier, they searched for more complex kinds of evil.

The hunter was an old curmudgeon, but he was not a real villain. He had tried repeatedly to kill the fox, but his true nature came out after the fox had saved him from the bear. The bear was the most fierce menace, even though he was not a true villain either, just a big, powerful animal who was angered.

5
The
New Era
Begins

The Black Cauldron

BY THE EARLY 1980s, THE STUDIO was a changed place. All of the supervising animators were gone except for Eric Larson, who remained only in a consulting position on animation and drawing. Morale was low, with small groups of artists trying to push scattered ideas for expanded opportunities and procedures to develop the new talent. In the animation department three disgruntled employees became a disruptive element, choking the creative spirit and group effort needed to produce the pictures. Then rather abruptly they left, and although harmony and growth began returning, it was still a troubled time. Some strength remained in story, but without a producer with vision or directors with experience, there was little chance of creating any richly entertaining product.

The studio had bought the rights to a series of books written by Lloyd Alexander that were quite popular with teenage readers. They were called the Chronicles of Prydain, and of the five in the series, *The Black Cauldron* offered the greatest potential of any story we had considered since Walt's death. It combined the humor, compassion and boldness of the

The Horned King plans to rule the world with his army of deathless warriors that was created in the Black Cauldron.

Model sheet of the furry little creature known as Gurgi. Lloyd Alexander who wrote the original story saw Gurgi as a high-level animal who desperately wanted to be human.

The king astride his horse has a threatening appearance, combining fantasy and mystery.

seven dwarfs from *Snow White* with the awesome and menacing dramatics of "Night on Bald Mountain," the personality relationships of *The Jungle Book* with the hilarious moments from *Peter Pan*. Here was a story that might pull the studio out of the doldrums and rebuild the enthusiasm that had been lost.

As a fantasy tale of legendary Welsh history it was ideal for the animation medium, especially in the visual potential for the scenes of the villain, the Horned King, and the frustrating attempts to battle his deathless warriors. It was all there in the original books.

The lack of experience in each department from producer to animator was quickly evident. Ron Clements, who was moving from animation through story to direction at the time, said, "This was to have been our *Snow White*, but we weren't ready for it." It was a sad misadventure. None of the author's spectacular ideas were understood and Walt's insistence on involving the audience by letting them see the emotions of the cast in every situation had been forgotten.

Typical of the failings, the Horned King, who should have been mysterious, was as ordinary as the leader of a street gang. As Roy Disney said later, their approach was "too literal-minded. He was just a guy." The use of close-ups and too much activity gave the impression that here was a man one could argue with. He should have been as unreachable and intimidating as Chernobog. No one should speak in his presence. The words should wither in one's throat. We should not even know if this evil creature was man, animal or demon. Here was unlimited power on the verge of taking over the world that somehow had to be stopped, and that was the special challenge to the tiny band of characters who carried the hopes of the future on their uncertain shoulders. It seemed an impossible burden for the heroic cast as well as the inexperienced staff at the studio.

There was some fine animation by the artists, who have since become tops in their field, but as all animators learn, the greatest animation in the world cannot save weak

story construction or overcome the failure to develop characters who are believable and enjoyable. The costs soared as the men in charge kept trying to pump in more effects, new visuals, more startling staging and more spectacle.

This was the situation when Roy Disney, son of Walt's brother Roy, helped mastermind a management change at the studio in 1984. He brought with him Michael Eisner, and Frank Wells as top administrators and Jeffrey Katzenberg as head of production. They were dismayed when they saw the nearly completed *Black Cauldron*. Their experience had all been in live-action films and animation seemed like an impossibly tedious way to make a picture. They recognized the weaknesses in the story, but they were several years from learning how to keep an animated film moving by intensifying the situations

The young hero, Taran, and his half-human companion, Gurgi, confront the Horned King. Instead of a powerful ruler, the King was treated as just an unpleasant man.

171

The Horned King leads his army in a devastating attack. One conceptual artist successfully combines imagination, mystery, and magic but it still emphasizes horror and despair over personality and story.

and building the characters' reactions. It was also too late to add the humor, the pathos and the fantasy which had been so strong in Lloyd Alexander's writing. The story had been a once-in-a-lifetime opportunity and it was heartbreaking to see such wonderful material wasted.

When completed, the audiences felt that *The Black Cauldron* was pretty, but confusing and overly somber. It had cost close to $40,000,000, an astounding price for an animated feature. It did not recover its cost in the theaters.

The portrayal of the Cauldron Born is more grisly than imaginative in its treatment of these warriors.

The Great Mouse Detective

Jeffrey Katzenberg, now chairman of Walt Disney Studios, and Roy Disney, vice chairman of the board of the Walt Disney Company, inherited one other picture from the previous management that would cause them problems. It was a picture that had been planned to be quite different, light and fun-filled, with whimsy and charm, and largely influenced by the popularity of the British comedy group Monty Python. It was based on the stories by Eve Titus about Basil of Baker Street, a mouse who lived next door to Sherlock Holmes and shared many of his traits and talents. There was a villain who was known as Ratigan, a takeoff on Moriarty, Sherlock's nemesis, and there was a mystery to be solved and a gang of villains to be caught. The story had all the right elements: the characters had the necessary appeal; the plot was one that could be easily handled with animation; and everyone felt that while it was not powerful it

would be a happy picture filled with the old values that had made the Disney films so successful.

They had the problems that haunt the production of every film, however, and there was still much to be learned. For one thing, the audience never had a chance to know the characters or their relationships before the story was off and running. In addition, the animators were having their troubles establishing the crucial personalities through the acting. Veteran animator Tom Sito claimed that the earlier animators had achieved a fine ability to "grasp the acting in a scene. . . . They could synthesize a performance into two key poses. This is what the animators of this generation lack. They have characters flapping their arms around, mugging and doing all these superfluous gestures and not communicating their ideas." Overacting and lack of focus have always been problems with lesser actors in the theater.

The personality of Ratigan, the villainous leader of the rat pack, had come not so much from the demands of the story but from a provocative photo found in an old book. Supervising animator Glen Keane told of how he was thumbing through these "photographs of people in London in the 1800s, of railroad men, and there was one guy smoking a cigar — he had a top hat and there was just something about this guy — this Ratigan . . . this rat sucking the cigar, completely dressed to the hilt, he was sharp and perfect — he's a sewer rat dressed like a

Master criminal Ratigan is the head rat, big and strong, with expensive tastes and a mean mind.

The original title, *Basil of Baker Street*, gave no indication that it was a story about a mouse who lived in the shadow of Sherlock Holmes, so the name was changed to the more specific, *The Great Mouse Detective*. A storyman quipped, "They could do that to every film we've made. Cinderella would be *The Girl in the See-through Slippers*."

Ratigan shows his growing disappointment when the mechanical toy in his hand will no longer function.

Ratigan is emotional and theatrical and has complete confidence in his ability to avoid being caught and to also rid himself of Basil forever.

king and he lives as a king!"

Glen came up with another procedure which added to the believability and dimension of his character. He explained: "I wrote a history of Basil as a child and Ratigan as a child. What kind of a kid was Ratigan? Why did he end up going this path? What was it like at home for him? In animating it, it just felt like you were spending some time with this guy — you weren't just plopping down at this point in history as if there never had been years before."

Once again Jeffrey Katzenberg and Roy Disney tried to breathe more excitement and tempo into this mild-mannered story. They changed the name to *The Great Mouse Detective*, which

Olivia, one of the victims of Ratigan's actions.

The peglegged bat, Fidget, does Ratigan's dirty work. He is evil and cruel, reasonably smart and very capable, but he leads an insecure life trying to constantly please his boss.

was certainly more provocative than *Basil of Baker Street.* Jeffrey was sure that a way could be found to systematize animation, as in a live-action film, keeping the cost down and properly preparing the material. Storyman Vance Gerry recalled the problem: "The best things in the [older] pictures didn't have much to do with the story. Those were the things people remembered and they [the story crew] should be trying to get these things, and if you did get it, it was one of the first things Jeffrey cut out because it was too vague."

Both Jeffrey and Roy knew what they wanted and what the picture needed and it was frustrating trying to find the places that could be patched up to make it all more interesting and exciting. They cut out slow spots, giving up quaintness and subtleties in order to keep the tempo from sagging, but they could not add the extra entertainment that was needed.

Several years later Jeffrey summed up his reactions to the finished film this way: "Everything about *The Great Mouse Detective* is at a level of 80%. Everything about it is pretty good as opposed to GREAT. For instance, Ratigan is intimidating — but not intimidating enough. The music is passable and the characters are . . . not accessible enough. The story — a good story, not great." Then he hastened to add: "I don't want to sound disrespectful to the movie, because I think we couldn't be

where we are today without it. That movie is part of our learning curve." Then he added *Oliver & Company* as another important "learning" film, and concluded: "Without those movies, we wouldn't have *Little Mermaid*, and *Beauty and the Beast*, and *Aladdin.*"

The archcriminal and fast-talker has no trouble making Basil look foolish.

177

Who Framed Roger Rabbit

The audience reaction to *The Great Mouse Detective* was not strong and the future of animation at the studio did not look bright. The new administration was enjoying phenomenal success with live-action films, and cartoon features seemed just too ponderous, too slow, too confusing in production, to attract much interest. A producer could not see the film that had been shot the day before in order to judge the progress, and more than that, the acting and the character were both locked inside some animator's head and who could tell what was going to come out.

Then in 1988 came *Who Framed Roger Rabbit*, bursting with energy, new ideas, old-style animation, robust and crude, but full of vitality. Here were realistic-appearing cartoon characters walking about in a human world. This concept would possibly have caused a difficult shift in techniques and entertainment values for a Disney-trained crew, but the studio management decided to make it a co-production with Stephen Spielberg and signed Robert Zemeckis to direct. Even the animation director, Richard Williams, had never worked in the Disney Studios. He had grown up on our films but

Roger screams at his private eye, "The cops are on our tail!"

The detective, Eddie Valiant, stands beside Roger's human-size sweetheart, Jessica. Problems of three-dimensional drawing, shading, and texture develop when a cartoon character is this large.

Each of the characters was a general type rather than an individual personality. Much of the time the live actors appeared to be unsure of how everything would look combined on the screen, but it didn't matter. It was a new type of entertainment and immensely successful.

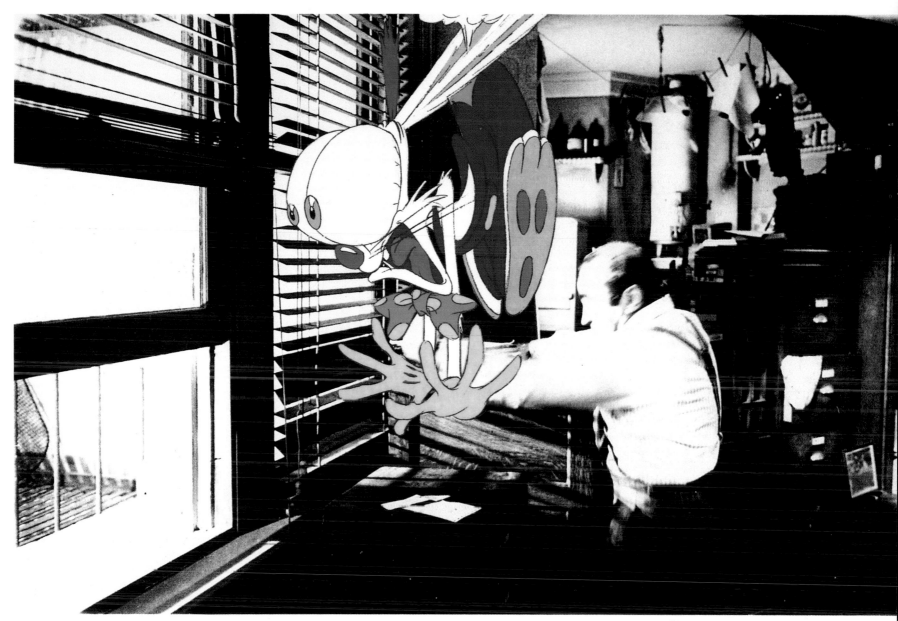

established his studio in London, where he dreamed of one day creating a feature film based on exaggeration, innovation and zany characters.

The story was a parody of the popular Humphrey Bogart films about jaded detectives in Raymond Chandler stories from the 1940s, with a script based on a wild, frantic victim trying to keep from getting killed. The live-action villain and his henchmen were caricatures, stereotypes, cold and heartless, with no real personality development. All of that went to Roger Rabbit and the second-rate detective who was trying to help him. There was no need for a character who was constructed with believable actions or one that

had won the audience's heart. This left the way open for fantastic gags and broad, slapstick animation. The audience loved it.

The picture brought a renaissance in animation throughout the industry and particularly sparked interest in that medium at Disney. The new stories that were put into production, however, were an outgrowth of the kind of films we had previously done. Jeffrey Katzenberg was determined to find a way to make an animated film that had warmth, romance and vibrant relationships between believable characters. It did not come easily, but new types of villains with all manner of entertaining victims were finally on their way.

Cartoon distortion widely used in the 1930s was brought back for this film. It was accepted more readily by today's sophisticated audiences than such action had been at the time.

Oliver & Company

The first picture was a new version of *Oliver Twist* with a cast of dogs, humans and one lone kitten. Charles Dickens had filled his original story with scruffy criminals, riverbank thugs and a gang of juvenile pickpockets under the command of a sly, scheming crook known as Fagin. There were enough villains in that book for several stories. In the studio's script for *Oliver & Company*, there were still strong elements of story and characters, and even good opportunities for songs, but not as many villains. It was a staggering assignment for the new director, George Scribner. Oliver was the kitten and the band of youthful criminals were street-smart dogs who made up the Company. The shrewd, master criminal, Fagin, was demoted to a simpering, small-time thief who had trained his dogs to be pickpockets, but he did not mistreat them in any way. Actually, he showed affection for them, even reading them a bedtime story.

The villain was Sykes, who had been elevated from the ruthless and stupid Bill Sykes to a powerful boss controlling every part of his empire. He was drawn in the best comic-book tradition, a big, blocky man with a square jaw and a square face seated behind a square desk in a huge warehouse surrounded by electronic warning systems. At first, the story crew thought he should be a mysterious, evil

The soft-hearted Fagin reads a bedtime story to his dogs.

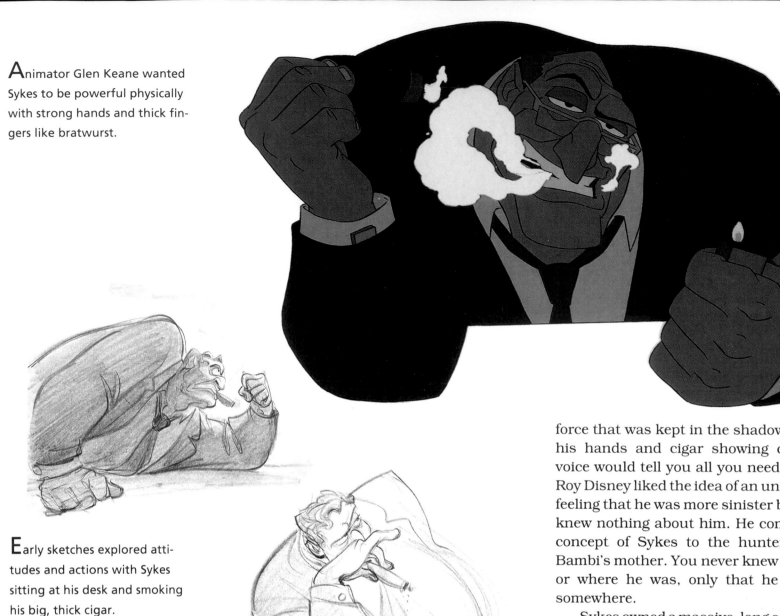

Animator Glen Keane wanted Sykes to be powerful physically with strong hands and thick fingers like bratwurst.

Early sketches explored attitudes and actions with Sykes sitting at his desk and smoking his big, thick cigar.

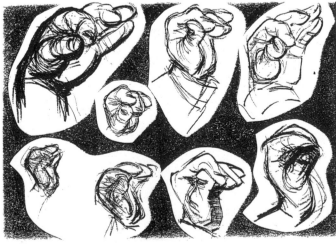

Animator's sketches of big hands and stubby fingers show type of research needed just for Sykes's hands.

force that was kept in the shadows with only his hands and cigar showing clearly. The voice would tell you all you needed to know. Roy Disney liked the idea of an unseen villain, feeling that he was more sinister because you knew nothing about him. He compared that concept of Sykes to the hunter who shot Bambi's mother. You never knew who he was or where he was, only that he was there, somewhere.

Sykes owned a massive, long car, all black, that seemed to typify his character. When he drove up to Fagin's place to collect the money owed him, neither the audience nor Fagin could quite see him. Slowly, the car window rolls down, Fagin leans forward with an alibi and is greeted by a puff of cigar smoke in his face. Sykes owns everything, even the people who work for him.

The story development called for more and more action for Sykes, however, and the concept of keeping him in the shadows had to be abandoned. Glen Keane was disappointed in the way this massive man looked when he had to move about like an ordinary person. "There was some stuff in the warehouse where he walks down the hallway, you wished you hadn't seen him walk around when he did."

There was no denying, however, that the

ending required an active, powerful, exciting villain, physically trying to accomplish what he had failed to do sitting behind his desk. Jeffrey Katzenberg spoke enthusiastically about this section. "You could see his rage, he is a very threatening presence. In fact, that last chase in the subway is what works best about the whole movie. All of that gets pretty scary!"

Vance Gerry had been called back from retirement to help develop the story. "I worked with Katzenberg," he said, "much closer than previous producers. [He was] much more knowledgeable about what works and what doesn't work, what he wants done and doesn't want done, frame by frame and sequence by sequence, he's right there." Vance went on to tell of the problems, "He didn't want to see storyboards — all those beautiful boards we'd worked out showing how the characters were going to work. 'Don't want to see it. Let's talk about what we're gonna do.' He wanted a script, something he could take home and read."

Vance concluded: "When it was all done, it was the picture that Jeffrey had described, a modern, up-to-date picture with a lot of modern, up-to-date music. . . I like to work with Katzenberg."

Who was the victim of Sykes's villainy? He hardly even saw Oliver. Was it Fagin? Or the little rich girl who wanted Oliver? Or the company of dogs who tried to protect the rest of the cast? A picture often flounders when there is no clear victim or even a hero to take on the villain.

Sykes controlled everything in this world he had built; nothing was left to chance. He had the power and many evil ways of hurting people. Here the little heroine Jenny is his victim

Fagin pleads for more time to pay his debt but he gets no sympathy from Sykes.

The Little Mermaid

While the animation department was busily trying to complete *Oliver & Company* by the imminent deadline, Ron Clements and John Musker, the two directors of *The Great Mouse Detective* were working on an adaptation of Hans Christian Andersen's beloved story "The Little Mermaid." There had been astounding growth in every branch of the department from computer-generated images to the finest character animation. There was also a villain in this new picture that would take her place alongside the greatest villains the studio had ever created. In the polls that showed Cruella De Vil as the most popular villainess of all our pictures, Ursula came in a close second.

Ursula had an unusual visual advantage over most other villains; she was an octopus. A creature of the sea, swimming, floating, moving in a sensuous fashion, ideal for an ominous, hypnotic type of schemer. When supervising animator Ruben Aquino started work on this character, he found that the extensive story sketches concentrated more on facial expressions than actions. Ruben said, "Actually it was Roy [Disney] who pushed for us to get more of that octopus feeling."

Roy had directed several of the nature films that followed the *True-Life Adventures* when he worked on production at the studio, one of his first being *Mysteries of the Deep*. He recalled: "It had a lot of octopus footage in it that I remembered, so when Ruben started doing this I said, 'You really need to study how they move, because the muscles aren't where you think they are. The muscles are way up in the body of the thing and that's why the tentacles move.' So he and I had a lot of fun trying to make it work."

There was some feeling that Pat Carroll's strong, no-nonsense delivery of the lines in Ursula's song would not fit the undulating, gliding movement of the real octopus, so they tried a simple test. Alongside the sound track of Pat's singing they ran a section of their live-action film of the octopus. To everyone's delight, it worked well and was both surprising and entertaining. With this assurance, all the animators working on the character used more of the realistic actions, which added much to the sinister personality and her fascinating movements.

Ursula is tough, crass, jaded, hard, and always looking for an advantage. When we first see her in the film, we are appalled at her appearance, and realize

Ursula became one of the studio's most popular villains.

Ursula watches Ariel in the magic mirror and sees the opportunity she has been waiting for.

The voice of Pat Carroll was perfect for this character with the right balance of shrewd persuasion and colorful expression.

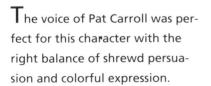

With her magic, Ursula has transformed herself into a lovely maiden complete with Ariel's voice, but her reflection in the mirror will not change. It is still the same ugly Ursula.

Ursula shows a magical image of Prince Eric to Ariel in order to acquire the girl's enchanting voice in return for three days on land as a human with the chance to win the Prince's love.

The Seattle Aquarium acquired a new female octopus and to get some publicity, had a contest to find a name for her. "Ursula" won easily since *The Little Mermaid* had been running in that area shortly before. But just weeks later the biologists informed the startled staff that they had just determined that the octopus was a male! Should they have a new contest? Admit the error? Hide the octopus? Keep the name and say nothing? They decided to simply abbreviate the name to Ursa which they hoped would satisfy everybody without raising questions. It worked, but they did not feel entirely right — fortunately, they received a good offer from another aquarium to buy the octopus so they sold it quickly. They held off the queries of the children of Seattle with some half-truths and began a search of their own for a new octopus that could be properly identified.

The little mermaid had to watch out for the shark, but more dangerous were Ursula's two eels who roamed the sea, searching for news, gossip and potential victims.

that here is someone to be reckoned with, but have no idea what she might do. Actually, she is brooding about the fact that King Triton has the power and the fame while all she has is a handful of victims transformed into helpless polyps. This is a very intriguing beginning — somewhat like a spider waiting for some unsuspecting fly to wander into her web.

The little mermaid, Ariel, is the ideal victim for this domineering female, who can soothe, cajole, feign sympathy, be helpful. Ursula also has magic at her disposal, potions one can drink, visions of the future one can see, and her song of the wonderful things that can happen for Ariel is more than this girl had ever hoped for. Who could resist this seasoned salesperson who knows every angle to pursue, every approach to spinning a cruel web about her victim?

Ariel is vulnerable and the viewers agonize over every step as they see their heroine gradually succumb to the tantalizing proposals. The crafty Ursula offers the sad girl three days to live on land and win Prince Eric's love;

if she fails, she will return to the sea and be under Ursula's power forever. The price is small, nothing really, only her voice! Ursula knows that the girl's father will do anything to save his daughter from such a fate, even to giving up his kingdom. Ursula will win, and the audience knows she will. This villain is a professional.

In the end, the audience has thrilled to a stirring presentation of heart tugs and heroics. Moreover, the animator has had the greatest opportunity for acting and personality development he will possibly ever have. As Ruben said, "A plum assignment fell into my lap!" (Three other animators shared in that plum, but Ruben had the responsibility and about half the footage.) He recognized that the voice of Pat Carroll was a very inspiring part of the task. "I didn't have to work hard to try to figure out what kind of acting to do."

Roy Disney compared her to Cruella: "Ursula was the same way in that she was a villain but she had that humorous kind of underpinning to where there was entertain-

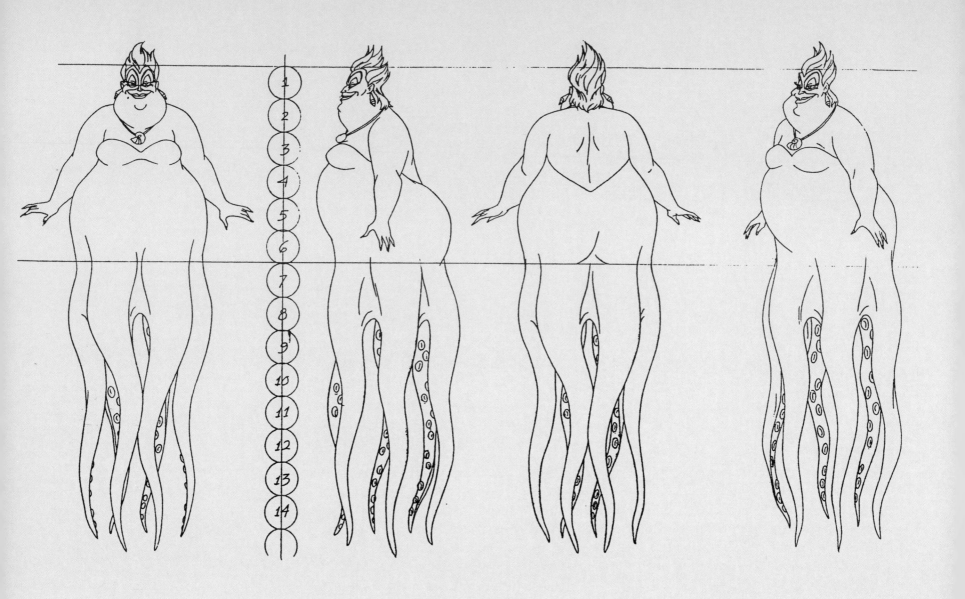

Final model of Ursula,
the octopus.

ment as well as the villainy. So it wasn't just all evil like Maleficent, where's there no redeeming anything, or the queen in *Snow White*."

Ursula's henchmen, the two eels, were particularly good because they reflected the slimy kind of sleaziness that we never actually saw with their boss. No one would ever trust that kind of scoundrel, which made them play well with the lovely, lonely mermaid. She looked so innocent and pure next to them that the audience understood immediately how distraught she was to even talk to these creatures. A strong bond with the audience came from the warmth generated by the girl's trying so hard to get what she wanted. Our hearts went out to her and we were deeply involved with everything she did. It was a prime example of how the villain and the victim help build the personality of each other, making both richer and stronger.

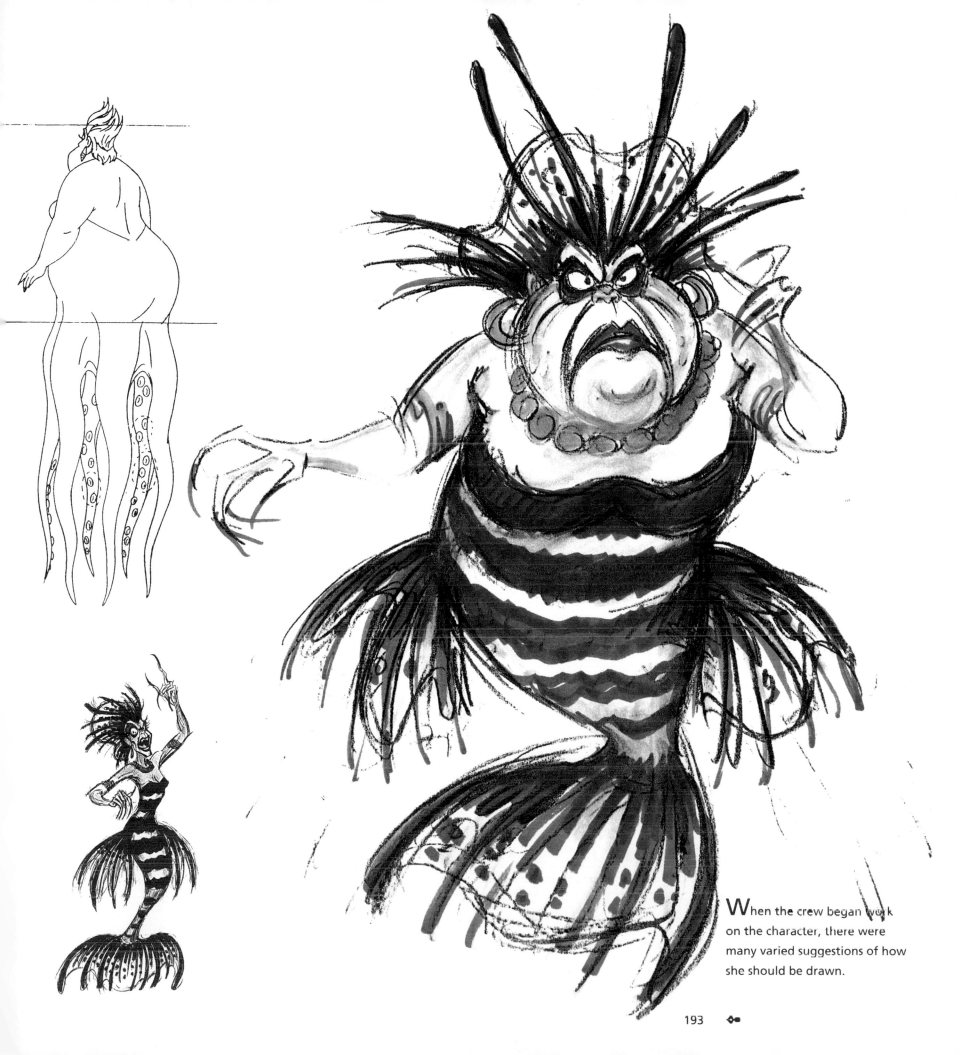

When the crew began work on the character, there were many varied suggestions of how she should be drawn.

The Rescuers Down Under

The time had come to make a whole production with computer-generated visuals from simulated action to ink and paint. There would be no more troublesome and expensive work on cels. It would all be done electronically. The film was *The Rescuers Down Under*, a fast-paced adventure sequel to the popular picture *The Rescuers*, which had been released in 1977.

From the beginning, the computer dominated the concept of the whole production, propelling the trend toward live-action thinking and planning in both individual scenes and story development. This made an additional challenge for the two directors, Hendel Butoy and Mike Gabriel, who had come up through animation. In contrast to the outstanding drawing of the flamboyant Medusa (the dazzling villainess in our first film about the Rescue Aid Society), the villain in this sequel, Mr. McLeach, was based on sketches of George C. Scott while he was recording the voice.

Three animators who were allowed to draw during the session captured in pencil lines the essence of Scott's expressions and attitudes, creating a more natural look than the usual adaptation of a character through refined caricature. Instead of a pliable face that could stretch and twist as it moved from one exaggerated expression to another, this face was lean and leathery, angular and bony, with no soft flesh to show elasticity in movement. McLeach was drawn like his car, which was hard and tough with sharp angles, but it was a difficult design for fluid animation.

Duncan Marjoribanks, the lead animator on McLeach, had asked for the assignment because he felt that "villains are intrinsically interesting – their motivations are really clear." This one had been conceived as a

The villainous Mr. McLeach, illegal trapper of rare animals. Character sketch by Mike Gabriel.

Sketches of George C. Scott as model for McLeach.

sadistic psychopath but Scott's voice was adding a broader range to the personality. Duncan thought that Scott might give some insight into how he envisioned McLeach and tried to involve him in a discussion by asking what had attracted him to the part in the first place. Rather than disclose any secrets of his own artistry, Scott quipped, "The money! I have three ex-wives to support, you know."

When the film was completed Duncan felt that McLeach did not quite come off the way he had hoped. "I did have a hard time getting into the character of McLeach. . . I might have staged him scarier, I might have loosened up the character design a bit too."

That design was equally inhibiting in helping to build a menacing villain-victim relationship with the boy, Cody. The two characters looked as if they came from different pictures, and while McLeach was strong-willed and frightening, it was difficult to care enough to become really concerned or involved. Not enough had been done in the story work to make the boy an appealing character or a sympathetic victim, and McLeach was not quite convincing as an interesting, spellbinding member of the cast. He was harsh, mean and capable, which presented an almost insurmountable problem for the mice trying to rescue Cody. He was an evil force that all the animals had to fear, but he lacked that touch of charisma that would hold an audience. Just being a bad guy is often not enough.

Joanna, the wild and scatterbrained lizard who would eat anything, was an added problem for all the animals, and especially the mice. She added a touch of excitement to events that were otherwise too predictable.

Surprisingly, it was the computer-generated half-track desert vehicle that provided the most ominous moments. It had a presence and a sound that could not be ignored. It would have been impossible to animate in one drawing after another, but it was the sort of action that today's computers can handle easily. It became the most villainous device in the picture.

teeth

chin

69

McLEACH - 3 McLEACH - 2 McLEACH - 1

36

McLeach was a crude, no-nonsense type of villain, short on compassion or concern, long on authority and being sullen.

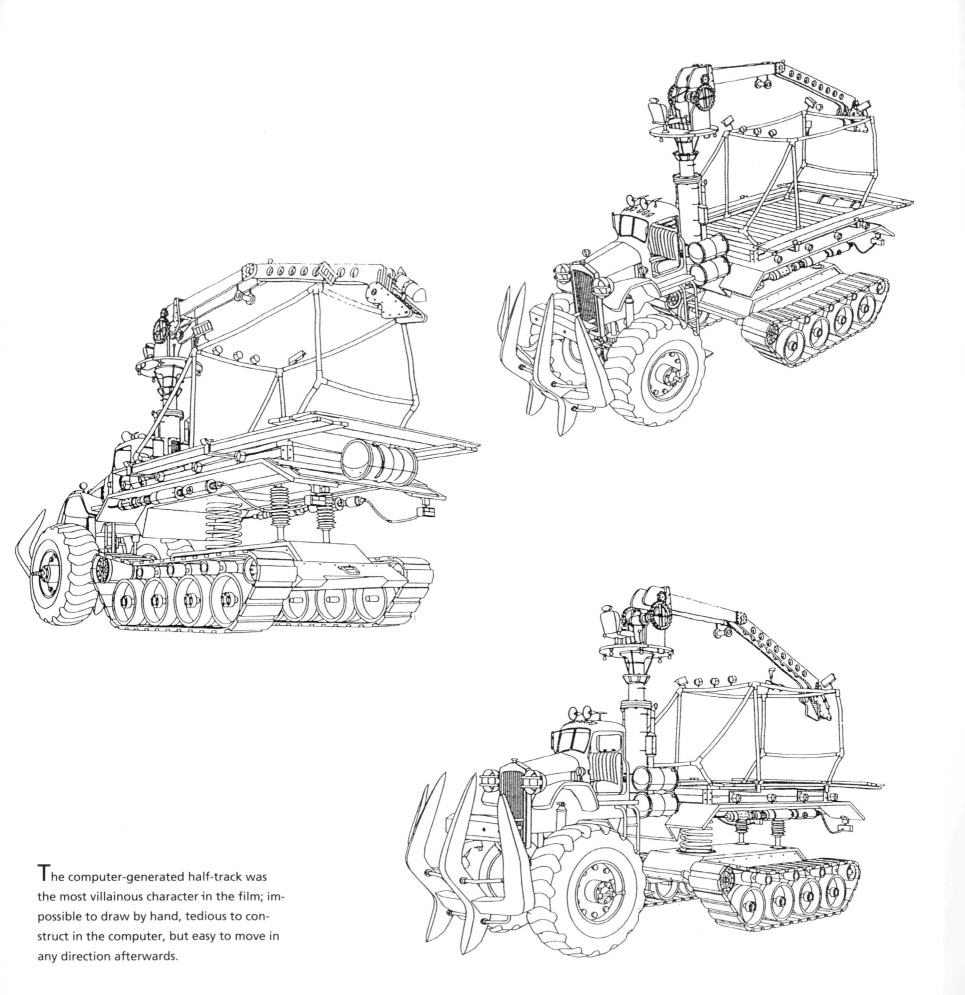

The computer-generated half-track was the most villainous character in the film; impossible to draw by hand, tedious to construct in the computer, but easy to move in any direction afterwards.

Jeffrey Katzenberg was impressed by the quality additions that came from the computers, saying, "I think *The Rescuers Down Under* is a spectacular, spectacular movie . . . And I think frankly a lot of the success we have had recently in these movies has been that we have had very strong villains. . . . Ursula is a great villain, and I happen to think that the George C. Scott character in *The Rescuers Down Under* . . . is a pretty nasty piece of work. Certainly not at the level of Cruella, but he is a pretty good bad guy."

McLeach was not quite alive in animation terms even though he was well-drawn and an interesting design, as in this sketch by Mike Gabriel. He needed more help in story and stronger situations for his acting to be as convincing as everyone had hoped.

Beauty and the Beast

Both Jeffrey Katzenberg and Roy Disney exclaimed, "This is no longer an animated cartoon! It's a real movie!" Their enthusiasm was confirmed when *Beauty and the Beast* was nominated for Best Picture of 1991 by the Academy of Motion Picture Arts and Sciences. It proudly took its place with the four other nominees, all live action. It did not win in the final voting, but no cartoon had ever been considered in this category previously.

The two directors, Kirk Wise and Gary Trousdale, were startled that their first efforts should receive such high honors. They had been hurriedly moved up from story when the first production crew had failed to capture the ingredients that Jeffrey Katzenberg wanted for this feature, and in spite of a late start, brought the picture in on schedule. With Jeffrey's participation, enthusiasm and conviction of what the film should be, they were lifted to a very enviable position. So after seven years of experimenting, learning, working together and understanding the animation medium, the management and staff of the studio had finally created a product that combined everything they had wanted in a picture. It had a strong story with a timeless theme, morality, romance, heart, memorable characters, excitement, live-action staging, timing and editing.

The characters were the most complex of any ever attempted in animation, with no one being a true villain until the final episodes. The character who appeared to be villainous at the beginning turned out to be a prince, and the most popular fellow in the town gradually became more and more villainous as he was thwarted in achieving his goals. The heroine was no damsel in distress and was never actually a victim of any villain. She was a modern, intelligent young lady who had taken charge of her own life. All three of them were far more true to life than to a fairy tale. As Alexander Solzhenitsyn has written, "If only it were all so simple! If only there were evil people somewhere insidiously committing evil deeds, and it were necessary only to separate them

Artist Glen Keane felt that the Beast was neither completely human nor all animal. When he is thoughtful, kind, and gentle, he expresses the finest human emotions. Glen claims he is the deepest character we have ever had.

The Beast could no longer be considered a villain after he had rescued Belle from the wolves in the woods.

The Beast is belligerent and antagonistic when he finds Belle's father wandering in the cursed castle.

from the rest of us and destroy them. But the line dividing good and evil cuts through the heart of every human being. And who is willing to destroy a piece of his own heart?"

Our earlier heroines for the most part were idealistic fairy-tale princesses trying to find and marry their storybook princes. They were living by their dreams and their wishes. Belle was more practical, liked to read books and was loving, helpful and protective of her aging father, who was no longer capable of caring for himself. When the Beast held the father hostage in a cold, damp jail cell, Belle made a bargain to take his place.

At this point the Beast was considered to be a villain by most people. The years of frustration and anger over being a captive in a hideous body had made him gruff and mean, with a terrible temper. As Glen Keane said, "He probably wouldn't have minded killing Maurice [the father]. That was the extent where someone like the Beast, who had the potential to be good, could become a villain. The Beast was pitying himself, frustrated, so he felt justified in treating the father that way, and when he comes back, Belle is crying — his actions do cause people pain — and he starts to get a glimmer that he's not entirely comfortable with the role of a villain.

When the Beast is angry, his animal instincts take over and he is totally a savage beast.

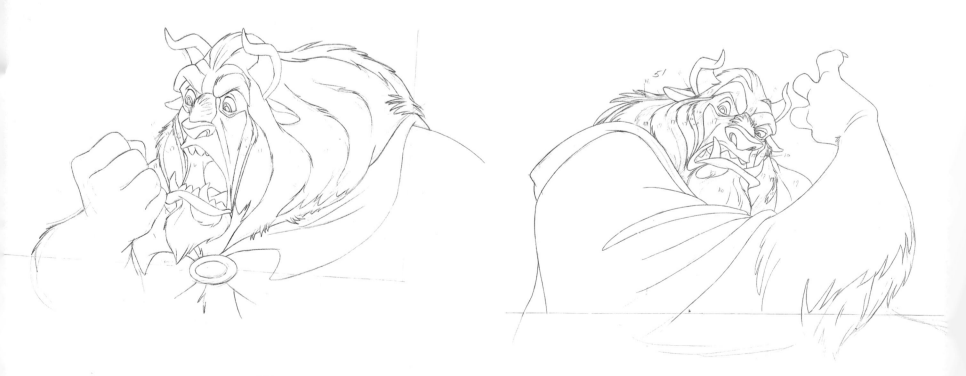

After Belle has been rescued from the wolves, a bond begins to grow between the Beast and the girl. Animator Ruben Aquino said that Glen Keane realized "whatever beast he came up with was going to be the definitive Beast, especially in the minds of kids growing up now. If they think about the Beast years from now, they'll think of his Beast. He knew that was quite a challenge."

Belle sees the Beast as a spoiled kid who grew up, and talks to him in human terms.

Early sketch of Beast as mandrill showing his human side, sad and concerned, wondering if he will ever be loved by anyone.

Gaston could not be a caricature of a country lout. He had to be a believable character with real personality development in order to be accepted as a true villain and the man who eventually murdered the Beast.

Gaston could be the he-man type found today, the egotistical weekend athlete who is convinced of his eternal popularity. Belle, however, is not impressed.

Frustration and humiliation has brought out the darker side of Gaston's personality. He realizes that in order to recapture his prominence in the village he must rid them all of the Beast.

The story sketch searches for dramatic staging and exciting visuals in telling the story. These drawings of Gaston and the Beast are not accurate models of the characters but are very stimulating as suggestions of how to use them on the screen. The drama of the fight on the roof of the Beast's castle is built with camera angles, startling silhouettes and imaginative use of the details of the buildings. There is no continuity at this stage, only inspiring possibilities. Story sketches by Vance Gerry.

. . . He had incredible limitations — it's kind of like taking the villain and the hero and wrapping them up into one body."

When the Beast sees Belle that first time, the question is raised: does he think she is the one who could lift the curse or is he just captivated by her manner and her beauty? Glen recalled the discussions: "We were constantly concerned about this fine line of him being sexually attracted to her — his eyes are reading into his mind that she's beautiful. He's lived in this lonely castle so long with his burden. 'Could she be the answer to my curse?' The other way was sort of this lecherous guy staring at her — this thought was amplified by the breathless voice asking, 'You would take his place?' It was a sensitive area probably dealt with too carefully and consequently not fleshed out as much as it could have been."

Roy Disney never felt that the Beast was evil. He said, "He's bad but he's not a villain. He's more like a little boy in a bad humor, you know — it's a sort of temper-tantrum thing." This was the attitude of the members of the staff at the castle who had been included in the spell of the curse. They knew the truth and helped us see a more sympathetic and pitiful side to the Beast. Under the influence of Belle, he quickly learned to be more civilized, eventually revealing a very sweet and considerate disposition. We understood why Belle fell in love with him.

Jeffrey Katzenberg explained that any movie can be beautiful and stunning, but if it does not have an emotional bell that rings "in a big-time way, everybody might as well go home. My point to Glen was that when the Beast is on the ground and his life is literally slipping away we, the audience, must believe that it is a tragedy. My challenge to him from the very beginning was: 'If you do not make me cry in this scene, then we will have failed to do justice to the literature — to the story.' "

Glen said, "I replied, 'Okay. I'm gonna try — I'm gonna try to make you cry.' I asked him at the screening, 'Did you cry?' He said he did."

The other male lead was the handsome, strong Gaston, the most popular man in

town. He was easily recognized by the viewers as a muscle builder in love with himself and they shared Belle's annoyance with his insulting behavior. To begin with, he assumed she would marry him, even without a proposal. Supervising animator Andreas Deja had started to draw Gaston as an arrogant, burly, mustached, self-acclaimed Romeo with a small brow and a large jaw. He was mainly a caricature, a buffoon and the butt of local jokes. It would be the "juiciest" animation assignment on the picture. However, Jeffrey Katzenberg insisted he had to be handled much more seriously or he would not be accepted as a villain. He should also be more handsome. Andreas thought, "Oh, my God, are we gonna have another prince?" He recalled the conversation. "I got really upset at the time because I had a crew of five other animators working with me and I didn't know how I could carry it through. . . Jeffrey was always saying when the girls see this guy on the screen, they should really fall for him, or feel that he's really gorgeous."

So off came the mustache and the big jaw and Andreas thought "soap opera handsome" as he drew. Jeffrey would explain: "I know it's more fun to animate the villain in broad, evil strokes, but what we're trying to convey is the important message of 'Don't judge a book by its cover.' You've got the girl in the middle and she has to make a difficult choice between the two 'heroes.' On one hand the Beast, on the surface, is very ugly, a monster, who we discover has some very human nice qualities. Gaston is the other pole — he's a new twist on the 'villain' part of our story . . . he's handsome and he's a real son of a bitch."

Obviously such a complicated character would have to be drawn more realistically in order to be convincing. Andreas felt that Hollywood was full of examples! Men who were always preening and putting each hair in place. "Sort of a modern kind of a guy. . . . It's not eighteenth century, it's really NOW. . . . You see these guys in clubs and restaurants and at the gym, of course. And then it starts to get a bit interesting. . . . How modern? And

Belle is too, in a way, being a girl who knows what she wants."

Roy Disney told of the problem convincing people that Gaston was the true villain in the story. "They say, 'No, he's not. He's just a stupid guy. . . He's like guys I know — he gets really bad at the end but all the way through he's just a "stupe" in love with himself.'"

The audience saw this too. In a theater, one girl said to a friend as the scene of Gaston proposing to Belle came up, "Oh, give me a break. I dated him a couple of years ago!"

However self-indulgent Gaston was, he was more of a bully than a real troublemaker. It was only when he was crossed in his desires that he felt forced to be more aggressive. Frustration and humiliation caused the major change in his personality, leading him to bribe a corrupt official to have Belle's father placed in the madhouse and later on to plot the killing of the Beast. He was never an admirable person, but he had not been a complete villain until the situation went beyond anything his limited talents could handle.

Undeniably, the realism of the characters in their occasionally fantasy backgrounds enthralled the audiences, and the live-action type of cutting quickened the tempo and gave new life to the telling of the story. The whole staff was naturally very proud and pleased with the enthusiastic reception *Beauty and the Beast* received, yet some of the artists were haunted by nagging doubts. A few complained that the main characters were only live-action actors dressed in animation drawings, with live action attitudes and mannerisms, all dealt with in a live-action handling of the story.

This had brought about a shift from fantasy to reality throughout. The characters were becoming stereotypes without the imagination that had brought forth Jiminy Cricket or Captain Hook or Prince John. One artist felt that the films had lost the magic of imagined relationships. They were almost like documentaries. "I think they are losing a lot of that sense of fun."

Inner struggle is the most difficult to animate of all the emotions in a picture. There is no strong action to draw, no acting that will communicate this turmoil, no change of expression that the audience can recognize. The artist in frustration usually pushes harder on his pencil, trying to force his character to reveal those hidden thoughts but that only makes matters worse.

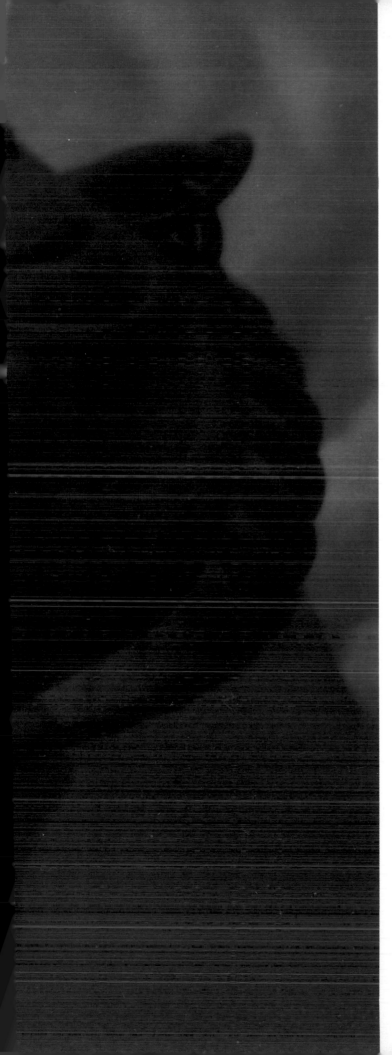

Aladdin

Roy Disney: "We're right back to Mr. Evil himself in Aladdin, you know. Jafar is just pure evil. He wants to take over the kingdom and kill everybody in sight or enslave them, or whatever suits his fancy."

Jeffrey Katzenberg: "Jafar is the most theatrical of the villains we have done to date. . . . I think Jafar is by far the best, most interesting, most maniacal, and most complicated, he's a great, great villain. . . This is the guy that wants it all. You know right from the start that he is a desperate character, capable of doing anything and everything to get what he wants."

There was high excitement at the studio even when Aladdin was only half animated. The story was essentially the familiar "boy meets girl, boy loses girl, boy gets girl," which had never been fully explored before in an animated film. It was convincingly done, and to the audience the boy-girl relationship was more important than the villain-victim development. It was a happy picture in which the dire deeds were more dramatic visuals than unnerving, life-threatening events, which added to the fun and excitement.

Jafar was using everything from his guards to his most potent magic to gain complete control of anyone who stood in the way of his plans. Aladdin was smart, quick and athletic, which kept him ahead of the palace guards, but more than that, he had a pet monkey who could go anywhere, get into any place and do whatever was needed to save his master. Just in case the monkey failed, there was the Genie in the lamp, with powers beyond anything on earth, who was always there to do Aladdin's bidding. Even Robin Hood did not have that kind of help.

The production staff was experienced and knew how to keep the villain just menacing enough to give believability to his actions yet bizarre enough to hold the audience's interest with something fresh and unexpected exploding in each situation. Jafar could have been played more seriously, but the picture would

A huge cat's head rises from the barren sands of the desert thanks to the modern computer capabilities.

The two romantic lovers who became the chief victims of Jafar's treachery. Jafar had no love for the Sultan's appealing daughter, Jasmine, but he needed to dominate her in order for his plans to succeed. Supervising animator: Mark Henn.

Jafar needed to kill Aladdin to get him out of his way. Supervising animator: Glen Keane.

not have been so bright and spirited. He was a storybook villain who did not have to prove how mean and odious he was.

Andreas Deja, who had given up his big-jawed design for Gaston on the previous picture, was given the animation assignment here. He said at the time, "I'm pretty happy with the design of Jafar after the Gaston realism. We came up with an Erté fashion design almost — very skinny, and he's got wide, padded shoulders and there's elegance to him. Long sweeping lines, so that just drawing-wise, it's so much more fun."

When he was asked if Jafar's movements would be restricted by that design, Andreas said the two directors, Ron Clements and John Musker, had told him, "Look at Maleficent — he's going to be really restrained and that's fine, that's all right." Strong design and controlled movement could add to the sinister aspect of the character, especially if his move-

Aladdin slips and falls during a bold effort to climb a wall.

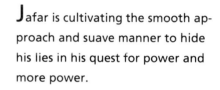

Jafar is cultivating the smooth approach and suave manner to hide his lies in his quest for power and more power.

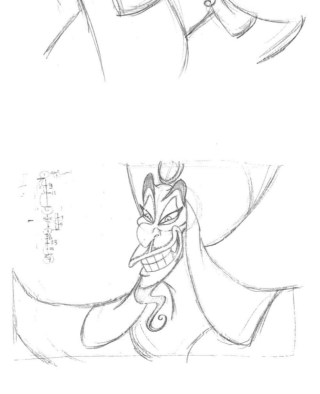

The animator, Andreas Deja, begins to study the expressions of people who are driven by excessive greed.

Jafar has acquired almost unlimited sources of magic and scarcely
needs any more, but his lust for
power drives him on.

Jafar is careful about who
he destroys since he needs
important people under
him in order to be a ruler.

Jafar was the perfect villain for this light-hearted, romantic tale of two young lovers caught up in adventures from literature. Story sketches by Ed Gombert (above) and Roger Allers (below).

Jafar

Aladdin

On this model sheet Andreas concentrates on showing a liar's face, the big, insincere smile, the ingratiating head and body moves.

ments maintained that same understated ominous quality.

Andreas saw a problem, however: "You look at the story reel and you see a guy digging in the sand, becoming hysterical, screaming at the parrot — he's pretty outgoing, so he's losing his temper quite often and then trying to control himself right after that and putting himself back together." These mercurial changes of moods make Jafar an interesting villain with a rich personality, but he does not evoke fear or hatred. The public taste in films has shifted from the deep, brooding, disturbing scoundrels to a lighter, fast-moving, shimmering type of character. (This is due partly to the younger age of the average audience, which demands more excitement, but also to the rating system, which often brands an action-packed film "Parental Guidance Recommended" because of its violence. The Disney studio cannot afford to have such a rating on its animated classics.)

When we asked Peter Schneider, president of feature animation at the studio, if he thought they could do another character as scary as the witch in *Snow White*, he answered, "I think times have changed since you animated the witch. We still try to make our films just as emotionally strong as you did but we have to be more careful. The witch today is probably a PG rating. We walk a difficult line in terms of how violent — not physically, but emotionally scary — a picture can be.

"You were emotionally scary in killing Bambi's mother. There's nothing about it that's PG but it is really frightening to have your mother killed. You've got to find the line to really scare people because I think it's okay to show evil in the world."

In the filmmaking business no one knows

it all and the wise producer, director, animator, will be modest and look for that bottle of "fairy dust" before claiming that he has another winner in his next venture. Still, it is obvious that in the years from 1984 to 1993 much has been learned at the Walt Disney Company and animation is alive and well and riding high. We can criticize and suggest and worry about missed opportunities, but we can also sit back and enjoy. The whole crew now knows how to put a picture together that will please audiences around the world. More than that, each film has different subject matter, types of characters and startling new visuals, and the expanding future holds even more promise of great things to come. We are proud of them and pleased to have been a part of such a unique tradition in the field of entertainment.

When Aladdin is in prison, a strange old man crawls in from a neighboring cell, offering a way to freedom. (It is really Jafar with another trick — it works!)

Jafar uses every trick and magical
device to get rid of Aladdin, but
the young hero is too agile. Sketch
by Roger Allers.

Jafar gets the Genie away
from Aladdin and is now truly
invincible.

He retains his poisonous personality when he changes himself into a mighty hooded cobra.

Aladdin and Jasmine share a magical moment of their own before Jafar becomes so powerful.

➥

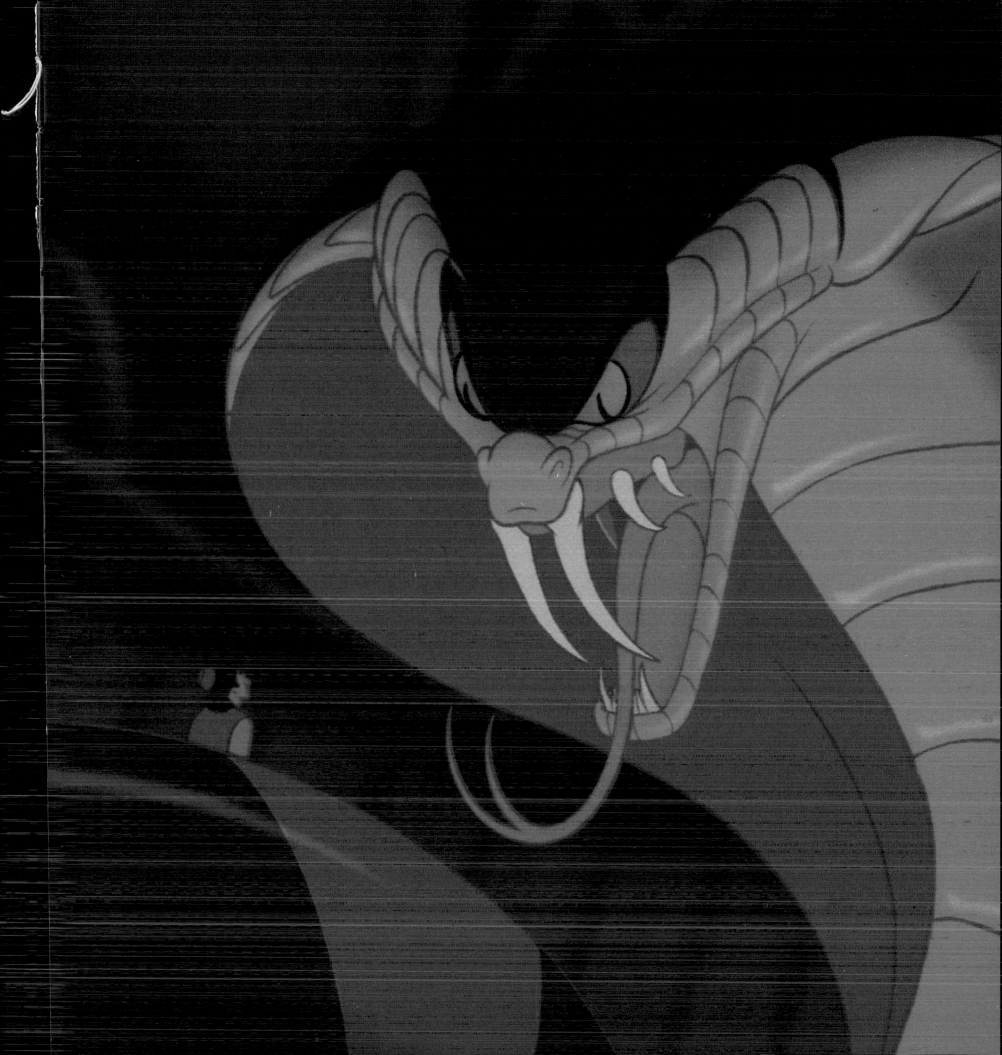

THE CREATORS

(the artists who animated the villains)

Norm Ferguson

Art Babbitt

Hamilton Luske

PICTURE	VILLAIN	ANIMATORS
Snow White and the Seven Dwarfs	Queen	Art Babbitt Bob Stokes
	Witch	Norm Ferguson Bill Roberts
Pinocchio	Fox & Cat	Norm Ferguson Hugh Fraser, John Lounsbery
	Coachman	Charles Nichols
	Stromboli	Vladimir Tytla
	Monstro	Wolfgang Reitherman, Vladimir Tytla
Fantasia	Chernobog	Vladimir Tytla
Bambi	Dogs	Retta Scott Worcester
	Fire	Dan MacManus

WAR YEARS

PICTURE	VILLAIN	ANIMATORS
Song of the South	Brer Rabbit, Fox & Bear	Ollie Johnston, Milt Kahl, Eric Larson, John Lounsbery, Marc Davis
The Whale Who Wanted to Sing at the Met	Professor Tetti-Tatti	John Sibley
Peter and the Wolf	Wolf	John Lounsbery, Ollie Johnston
The Adventures of Ichabod and Mr. Toad [Mr. Toad]	District Attorney Mr. Winkie Weasels	Ollie Johnston Rudy Larriva Hugh Fraser
[Ichabod]	Brom Bones Ichabod Headless Horseman	Milt Kahl, Ollie Johnston, Frank Thomas Frank Thomas, Ollie Johnston Wolfgang Reitherman John Sibley
Cinderella	Stepmother	Frank Thomas Harvey Toombs
	Stepsisters	Ollie Johnston Judge Whitaker
	Lucifer	Ward Kimball John Lounsbery, Phil Duncan

Vladimir Tytla

Fred Moore

Wolfgang Reitherman

Retta Scott Worcester

John Lounsbery

Charles Nichols

PICTURE	VILLAIN	ANIMATORS
Alice in Wonderland	Queen of Hearts	Frank Thomas Eric Larson
	Cheshire Cat	Ward Kimball John Lounsbery
Peter Pan	Captain Hook	Frank Thomas Wolfgang Reitherman
	Mr. Smee	Ollie Johnston Cliff Nordberg
	Crocodile	Wolfgang Reitherman Cliff Nordberg
Lady and the Tramp	Rat	Wolfgang Reitherman
	Aunt Sarah	Hal Ambro, Jack Campbell
	Siamese cats	John Sibley, Bill Justice, Bob Carlson
Sleeping Beauty	Maleficent	Marc Davis
	Goons	John Lounsbery
	Dragon	Wolfgang Reitherman Eric Cleworth
101 Dalmatians	Cruella De Vil	Marc Davis
	Horace and Jasper Badun	John Lounsbery John Sibley, Amby Paliwoda
The Sword in the Stone	Madam Mim	Milt Kahl, Frank Thomas
	Wolf in woods	John Lounsbery
	Pike in moat	John Lounsbery
The Jungle Book	Shere Khan (tiger)	Milt Kahl
	Kaa (python)	Frank Thomas, Milt Kahl
	Colonel Hathi (elephant)	John Lounsbery Eric Cleworth
	King Louie (orangutan)	Frank Thomas, Milt Kahl John Lounsbery
The Aristocats	Butler	Milt Kahl Frank Thomas, Julius Svendsen
Robin Hood	Prince John	Ollie Johnston
	Sir Hiss	Ollie Johnston, Frank Thomas Cliff Nordberg
	Sheriff	Milt Kahl John Lounsbery, Frank Thomas
	Nutsy and Trigger	Eric Larson, John Lounsbery

Ward Kimball

Eric Larson

Duncan Marjoribanks

Frank Thomas

Ollie Johnston

Marc Davis

PICTURE	VILLAIN	ANIMATORS
The Rescuers	Medusa	Milt Kahl
	Crocodiles	Frank Thomas, Milt Kahl
		Cliff Nordberg
The Fox and the Hound	Bear	Glen Keane
	Hunter	John Musker
		Jeff Varab, Andy Gaskill, Jerry Reese,
		John Lounsbery, Randy Cartwright,
		Chuck Harvey
The Black Cauldron	Horned King	Phil Nibbelink, Steve Gordon, Doug Krohn,
	Warriors	Ruben Procopio, Ron Husband
The Great Mouse Detective	Ratigan	Glen Keane
		Matthew O'Callaghan, Phil Nibbelink
Oliver & Company	Sykes	Glen Keane
		Tony Fucile
	Fagin	Glen Keane
		Ruben Aquino, Kevin Lima, Steve Markowski,
		Dave Stephan, Dave Cutler
The Little Mermaid	Ursula	Ruben Aquino
		Kathy Zielinski, Dave Cutler, Nik Ranieri,
		Rob Minkoff, Chris Wahl
	Vanessa (Ursula as girl)	Andreas Deja, Doug Krohn, Mike Cedeno,
		Chris Bailey, Kathy Zielinski
	Eels	Shawn E. Keller

Kathy Zielinski

Glen Keane

Andreas Deja

PICTURE	VILLAIN	ANIMATORS

The Rescuers Down Under	McLeach	Duncan Marjoribanks
		    Chris Wahl, Mark Henn, Roger
		    Chiasson, Ken Duncan, Ruben
		    Aquino, Phil Young,
		    Alexander Kuperschmidt

	Joanna (lizard)	Dave Cutler, Broose Johnson, James Baxter, David Burgess, Kathy Zielinski
	Bushwhacker (truck)	Eric Daniel, Scott Johnston, Tina Price, Andrew Schmitt, M.J. Turner

Beauty and the Beast	Gaston	Andreas Deja
		    Joe Haidar, Ron Husband, David
		    Burgess, Alexander Kuperschmidt,
		    Tim Allen

	Beast	Glen Keane
		    Anthony DeRosa, Aaron Blaise,
		    Geefwee Boedoe, Broose Johnson,
		    Tom Sito, Brad Kuha

	Wolves	Larry White

Aladdin	Jafar	Andreas Deja,
		    Nik Ranieri, Ken Duncan,
		    Ron Husband, Lou Dellarosa

	Jafar as Old Man and Snake	Kathy Zielinski

Milt Kahl

Ruben Aquino

227 ◄●

Index

Page numbers in *italics* refer to illustrations.